Snapping

Lines

Camino del Sol

A Latina and Latino Literary Series

Snapping
Lines

Stories by Jack Lopez

The University of Arizona Press

TUCSON

The University of Arizona Press
© 2001 Jack Robert Lopez
First Printing

♾ This book is printed on acid-free, archival-
quality paper.
Manufactured in the United States of America

06 05 04 03 02 01   6 5 4 3 2 1

Library of Congress Cataloging-in-Publication
Data
Lopez, Jack, 1950–
Snapping lines : stories / by Jack Lopez.
p. cm. — (Camino del sol)
ISBN 0-8165-2075-5 (alk. paper)
ISBN 0-8165-2076-3 (pbk. : alk. paper)
1. Hispanic American men—Fiction. 2. Hispanic
Americans—Fiction.
I. Title. II. Series.
PS3562.O67245 S63 2001
813′.54—dc21   00-009379

British Library Cataloguing-in-Publication Data
A catalogue record for this book is available from
the British Library.

Publication of this book is made possible in part by
the proceeds of a permanent endowment created
with the assistance of a Challenge Grant from the
National Endowment for the Humanities, a federal
agency.

for Pat & Denis

Snapping lines means transferring the blueprints to the slab. Incorrectly snapped lines throw off the entire project.

—Ricardo Means Solarzano

Contents

Snapping
Lines

In the South

I t was a warm spring afternoon, and Raymond watched the surf roll in from his vantage point on the cliff. The bathing beach was far below, littered with sunbathers and vendors, and a few people had ventured into the rough surf to escape the heat. Raymond, swathed in the gathering breeze, looked back toward the resort. Jill was in the bungalow. He'd tired of arguing with her, had tired of the long, unbroken silences in between each argument, so he'd begun his walk along the cliff.

When Raymond—actually Ramón, but for business reasons he'd added the y and d to make people more comfortable in their dealings with him and make him more comfortable in his dealings with them—married Jill more than four years ago, they had both agreed that should things go badly between them, should the relationship be at risk, they would spend a weekend together, away from everything. Things had indeed gone sour. Remembering his promise and keeping his word, because he *always* kept his word, he had suggested a resort on the Baja Peninsula, a place he remembered from his youth, one that was sufficiently far from accessible roads yet easy to get to by plane. So they had taken the "San Diegan" to the border and then a cab to the airport, where they had caught their flight.

Out in the bay one of the swimmers caught Raymond's eye. The bather, far out beyond the other swimmers, thrashed about. Something didn't look quite right, but he figured that in his present state of mind he was probably imagining things. Yet he couldn't take his eyes off the bather. As he looked out to sea, he saw a group of waves approaching larger than any of the previous. And now watching the swimmer in earnest, he really did sense danger, for the image of the swimmer had faded under water.

Raymond ran along the cliff until he was directly above a group of sunbathers. He yelled down to them, pointing to the ocean. They waved back. He flapped his arms above his head, trying to mimic the movement of swimming, and yelled as loudly as he could, finally realizing that the breeze was blowing every word back in his face and the sunbathers couldn't hear them. The people below soon lost interest in his antics and turned away.

The resort consisted of a large Mediterranean-style building, white with a red tile roof, surrounded by smaller cottages. The resort was built on a cliff; the only path to the beach was in front, and Raymond ran for it.

The first wave of the set completely engulfed the small swimming bay in a white explosion. Running, he felt just the slightest bit of movement in the ground from the breaking wave. He was scared; as he ran, his heart racing, he could no longer see the flailing swimmer. Giant combers pounded the bay, a maelstrom of silver, pristine white, and diamond-like reflections.

By the time he reached the sand the bay was calm, though still swirling with angry water, some of it milky green, some of it dark and sandy colored. Raymond discarded his sandals so he could run faster. His feet squeaked in the dry sand each time they hit, and except for the roar of the sea, everything was silent, almost cold. He tried to envision the last place he had seen the swimmer, sprinting until he felt satisfied with his point of reference in relation to the cliff. But you can never be sure.

Raymond told two children making sand sculptures to get the lifeguard (the resort employed two full-time lifeguards, or so it said in the brochure), told them what he'd seen. The children didn't react until Raymond removed his Guatemalan shirt and waded into the ocean, searching for any sign of the swimmer. After his short pants were wet and he had somewhat adjusted to the temperature of the surf, he dove in, swimming out to where he had last seen the bather. Almost immediately he felt himself in the grip of a tremendous rip tide, moving sideways much more rapidly than he moved out to sea. So he relaxed, waiting for breakers, and soon he was back in shallow water, but much farther south.

He stood ankle deep in wavelets, his hands shielding his eyes, trying to see movement in the shimmering, roiling ocean before him. But he couldn't. Hearing the siren of the lifeguard's jeep, he moved up to dry sand.

The lifeguards questioned Raymond, and he answered them as capably as he could. Soon every sunbather was involved in the search. They spread themselves along the shore, walking in and out of shallow water. One of the lifeguards went up on the cliff with binoculars.

At last in the evening, just before dark, Raymond saw his swimmer. She wore a dress. A festive red floral print one. How could he have known the swimmer was a woman?

Two teenaged boys dragged her from the surf at the south point of the bay. The boys handled her like baggage, dropping her on the sand, out of the water. Already a sand crab scurried over her neck. And her dress was hiked up above her thighs, so that you could see her pubic hair contrasted with her white underwear. Even though she was indigenous, from Baja California, her skin had a lighter tone to it, one that seemed strangely off. Her eyes were half open, her gaze to the sky. Raymond wanted to close her eyes, wanted to pull down her dress, but instead he turned away. It would be much too familiar for him to touch this drowned stranger. Instead, someone draped a beach towel over her, so that she was lost from sight, a bump on the sand, a tourist body hiding.

The resort manager was now on the beach, and he assured Raymond that "things" would be placed in order. He spoke to Raymond in Spanish, using the familiar *tu*. Raymond turned away from the manager, away from the small crowd and the woman's body, and stared out to sea. Even though the sun was gone, a few textured white clouds on the horizon showed pink on their edges.

"You did everything you possibly could," Jill said. She leaned on her elbow, lying on the bed with her legs covered by a white spread. Her eyes were puffy.

The curtains flapped in the evening wind. Raymond felt as if his eyes, too, should have been swollen, as if he should have cried, but he couldn't. He felt only emptiness. "But I didn't," he almost whispered. His throat ached. From yelling when he was on the cliff, he supposed.

Someone knocked at the door. Raymond stood up from the love seat at the side of the bed and slowly walked into the small sitting room. Each step he took felt heavy, leaden. He opened the door. A young waiter entered and set a tray on the wicker coffee table. Raymond signed the tab, tipped the waiter, then took the drinks into the bedroom. He gave the gin and tonic to Jill; he kept the double scotch.

Jill had removed the spread and sat huddled against the headboard with her legs drawn up underneath her. She wore one of those long, extra-large T-shirts with an emblem on the front, though Raymond couldn't make out exactly what the emblem was because only part of it was stretched across her knees.

"Do we drink to ends, then?" Raymond asked. He was thinking of the drowned woman, as well as his nearly failed marriage to Jill.

"Of course not! We drink to trying."

Raymond stood at the side of the bed. They clinked their glasses together. He took a gulp and then sighed. "I just feel like shit."

"I know," she said. "I know."

Raymond took another drink. He set his glass on the nightstand while sitting on the bed. Jill leaned forward, and they held each other. Off in the distance Raymond heard the sound of breaking waves, but he thought of the faraway look he'd seen in the swimmer's eyes, the look that seemed to be searching for something.

As they hugged, Raymond felt Jill's strong back. He ran his hands over her smooth legs, kissing her neck. She pulled him tightly into her.

Then suddenly remembering her infidelity, Raymond backed away. He reached for his drink, slugged it down, and said, "I'd better shower."

Jill exhaled hard, a hurt look crossing her face as she turned away from him, but he moved into the bathroom anyway.

He tried to cry while showering, but couldn't. His eyes clouded while he shaved, but that was the extent of it. Sometimes you don't have anything left—he'd done his crying long before this last-ditch effort to save the relationship, yet never once in front of Jill.

As Raymond re-entered the bedroom after bathing, he saw that Jill was already dressed for dinner. She wore her black Yohji Yamamoto suit, the one that was cut unevenly so that it looked like a huge, hip mistake. But on Jill it was no mistake. She knew how to wear it. She had the right body, a model's, except with weight in the right places, which was a contradiction because, of course, she wasn't really model-like. Had Raymond been able to choose what models looked like, Jill would be his ideal. No little boy/girl stuff. Women. Women with big thighs and women with real bodies. Jill had green eyes that contrasted wonderfully with her light hair. She thought her neck too long, her mouth too large, but Raymond thought these things all added up to true beauty, as nothing was predictable.

From the walk-in closet he took his black pinstriped suit because black was, after all, really the right shade for the state of things as they now existed.

After Raymond dressed, he and Jill walked among the bungalows to the resort restaurant. They didn't speak and they walked amid palm trees and climbing bougainvillea and even fir trees, the entire setting reminding Raymond of their honeymoon in Rome. A large moon, not full, highlighted the transplanted flora.

At the entrance to the restaurant, Jill took hold of his hand. She held it firmly, exciting him, but he stuck to his stubborn facade of indifference toward her. She finally let it go, following the maitre d' to their table.

"Pretend we're on a date," Jill said. "I know it's not festive, but we can still like each other."

Raymond pushed the chair in for her, waving off the maitre d'. Sitting in his own chair, he said, "That's the big problem." He felt much, much more than "like" for her.

"It doesn't have to be a problem."

Looking around the restaurant at the clusters of guests strategically arranged, he had a feeling of people, of a crowd, even though there were only four other parties. It was still too early in the season to be crowded, though in a week or two it probably would be. He thought he recognized a few people from the beach, but they were going about their business, eating and drinking as if nothing out of the ordinary had occurred. Weren't you supposed to be affected by big events? By death? By the breakup of your marriage? He somehow couldn't get it up to act out his role in the evening's entertainment.

"Sometimes it's a big problem."

"It doesn't have to be."

Jill stared in toward the lounge, where a band was setting up. She liked to dance, Raymond didn't particularly. He knew that the root of their problems lay in the fact that she was able to exist in the "now." Raymond was always either fretting about the past or worrying about the future. And that was his problem: He wasn't able to forget the past.

But how could he not like Jill? She was everything he needed. She was sexy at the right times, elegantly sexy. She was intelligent. She didn't bore him. In all his past relationships he'd ultimately become bored.

Had she been sexy in her affair? Other than saying that it had been with someone he didn't know, that it was over, that it had started because this man had taken an interest in her at a time when Raymond hadn't, she would give no concrete details, even under his most exacting interrogation.

The phone machine had given it all away. The message much too familiar, much too chancy. When he'd asked who'd left it, Jill hadn't hesitated telling him.

His energy had been violent for a time, and he'd stayed in a motel until he cooled. Jill said she wanted the marriage to work. Raymond still loved her.

"I want lobster." She stared at him.

He couldn't take her gaze, so he looked for a *mesero*. Instead, the sommelier approached, took their order, and then left them once again in solitude.

The band began tuning their instruments. Jill raised her eyebrows suggestively at Raymond and he couldn't help smiling at her.

"Was that so difficult?"

He nodded his head.

The wine steward returned and did his ritual with the corkscrew and cork; he let Raymond taste a small amount of wine, then filled their glasses. To coincide with the wine ritual, a *mesero* materialized and took their order.

"Don't make it so hard," Jill said after the waiter disappeared. "We're not enemies."

Raymond answered, "I don't trust you." Then, "I keep thinking of the drowned woman."

"Think of *me*. I'm here. I'm alive. We're married."

Raymond snickered. Was this how *gabachas* conducted their
marriages? In his own culture it was okay for the male to stray. Not
really okay, but it was done. He'd never known anyone in his boat.
He'd never known anyone who had to deal with his wife going out
on him. Raymond himself had had many opportunities to be with
other women had he desired, but he hadn't. He hadn't wanted to
hurt Jill. He'd kept his word.

"You broke your promise," he answered.

"So did you. Where were you? Where?"

That was a silly question. He was working, becoming a success,
assimilating, becoming a positive role model. "You know where I
was."

"You weren't there for me."

They had drunk most of the bottle of wine by the time their
dinner arrived. Raymond had trouble eating his food because he
kept thinking of lobsters as living in the ocean, and when he
thought of the ocean, he was reminded of the surf, and when he
thought of the surf, he saw the drowned woman. He couldn't figure out why she wore a dress. Such a festive one. He even specu-
lated to himself that she had worked at the resort. She was gone
now, so the speculation was really quite worthless. But it wouldn't
stop. He kept seeing her face, her skin almost glowing in the
gathering darkness, the white sand sticking to her wet legs. Finally
he pushed his plate forward.

Feeling very hot, unable to catch his breath, he said, "I've got
to get out of here."

Jill looked at him with concern and anger. "Thanks a lot."

"Finish your dinner. Listen to the music."

"Are you coming back?"

"I don't know. I don't know. I don't know!" The few people in the restaurant looked their way. Raymond, lowering his voice, said, "I need to walk."

"What about my needs? Our needs?"

Raymond was out of the restaurant, almost gasping for air. The sea breeze was stronger now, heavy with the smell of salt and ocean mist. He walked to the edge of the cliff and bent over, taking very deep and slow breaths. Soon his mind cleared somewhat.

He passed along the clifftop, away from the resort, to the place where he had first seen the swimmer. He gazed out over the bumpy, tinsel ocean, searching for her. He wanted a replay, another chance. He wanted to leap down the face of the cliff, dive into the sea, and power-stroke to the rescue. Or better yet, he imagined flying. Fly to where she thrashed, pluck her out of the water, and make things right.

He wanted to will her back, but of course he couldn't. He knew this. Yet he wondered if her spirit was still close, hovering over the waves, for when death is this palpable, you're supposed to feel something, aren't you?

All Raymond saw was phosphorescent explosions as the waves broke in rhythmic, cosmic beat. Over and over the breakers hit the beach. Over and over Raymond saw the woman, her dress, her color.

Losing track of time, and after staring at the black ocean for what seemed an eternity, he turned and began moving inland. He brushed and scraped through the chaparral, skirting the edge of the resort, walking all the way to the road that led out of town. He'd always been fascinated by those stories in which people simply wander off and assume new identities.

To the south the road was steep, a great, gradual incline. All around were hills and the natural brush of Baja California. Off in the distance he saw headlights approaching the upgrade. As the lights neared, Raymond heard the heavy grinding of gears as a truck downshifted, making the climb. It moved slowly and carried a strange cargo. A cargo that glowed. He knew that the moon cast an unpredictable light on things, but this truck actually glowed, the trailer giving off a blue light. He instinctively backed away from the road.

Suddenly the truck was upon him, rattling, swirling the dirt on the shoulder, creaking and groaning and roaring with mechanized fury. As the truck passed, Raymond saw that the halo surrounding it was created by ice. Tons of ice in the wood-slated trailer. And fish. Huge tuna with heads sticking up, dorsal and pectoral fins darting through the slats, all commingling with the ice.

In an instant the truck, the glow, the fish were all past him. Everything smelled dry. The stars seemed clearer, seemed to fill the sky so much that it might become overweighted and fall.

Even though he wasn't cold, Raymond shivered hard as goose bumps formed on his shoulders, traveling his spine to his lower back. He looked at his shoes. They were covered with dust. His suit slacks had burrs on them.

For some unknown reason he thought back to another time when he'd been far down in Baja California. He'd been a senior in high school and had come with friends, surfing. They explored many coves, driving for hours on dirt roads that opened onto the bluest sea that you could ever imagine, diamonds glistening off the swells. And they found one cove that offered almost perfect waves. They surfed all day, but when they returned to shore in late afternoon, there was a Volkswagen camper parked on the beach, something they hadn't expected—other people in their secret place.

The new arrivals were a couple, older than Raymond and his friends, though not by much. The couple spent most of the afternoon in the van, which inspired quite a bit of envy in Raymond because he just knew they were making love.

In the early evening Raymond approached the couple's campsite to offer them lobster that he'd bought earlier at a fishing village. The camper had an awning sticking out from it. A young woman sat under the awning on a camp stool, sipping hot chocolate and brandy (he saw the bottle of brandy and the chocolate on the camp table next to the fire), crying softly. "He won't come back," she said to Raymond.

Raymond looked to the surf, barely making out a shape entering the water.

"I dreamed it," the young woman said. She wore bathing suit bottoms and a white muslin peasant shirt. "He's not coming back."

Not knowing how to respond to the woman's statement, Raymond said, "We have some extra lobster."

"He got his draft notice and I dreamed his death and things will never be like this again."

Raymond felt extremely embarrassed for having intruded upon this couple's private anguish. There was a small war in Asia, and Raymond himself would soon enough be subject to the very same draft. But that was something he would contend with later. For now, he was a senior in high school on a surfing trip, trespassing on lovers.

He set the lobsters on the camp table. On his way back to his own campsite Raymond had passed the young woman's lover, returning from the sea. The man had nodded at Raymond in a serious yet knowing way.

Now, way up on a hill, in another galaxy, the glowing truck rounded a curve and was lost from view. Raymond was in motion once again, yet this time he was going back to Jill. He walked past his rented bungalow, all the way to the restaurant, quickening his pace as he neared. Inside, he searched for Jill, but she was no longer at their table. From the lounge he heard the band playing, so he entered. And there he saw her sitting in a large booth, alone. She gazed over the empty dance floor, her mouth set, the breeze from the open window at her back wiggling her hair.

Without realizing it, Raymond was leaning against the bar. Nobody else sat there, and only a few people occupied other booths in the lounge. The bartender asked Raymond what he wanted to drink. In spite of the fact that he'd barely eaten, he ordered amaretto. And he sat at the bar, watching Jill through the reflection in the mirror.

The band punched out a quickly paced *ranchera,* but there were no dancers to revel in the music. From a side door two men, American, entered the lounge, stopping before Jill. They smiled and spoke to her, but she remained impassive, sort of staring onto the dance floor. The bartender set down Raymond's liqueur. Jill shook her head in the mirror.

She claimed that Raymond hadn't been there when she needed him. Maybe she was right. Where had he been? How had Jill felt through all this? How much had she suffered? Was it possible that Raymond had been unfaithful, though not sexually? If all this was about betrayal, then it was certainly possible that Raymond had been a participant in some sort of fraud. He struggled, trying to make the right connections.

He watched her reflection in the mirror, saw the backs of two men who continued to speak with her in spite of no encouragement, and saw, too, the drowned woman, the ice-filled truck, the young woman who'd dreamed her lover's death.

He downed his drink, grimacing at the sweet heat that passed through his throat, swirled on his barstool, and quickly strode to the stage. To his surprise, the band stopped playing. Raymond made his request to the singer. Then he pushed between the two men at Jill's booth.

"Dance with me?"

"Did you commune with her dead spirit?"

"Don't be mean."

"I guess this was a mistake."

"No, it wasn't."

"You can't even eat with me. You can't stand the sight of me."

"You're important. Dance with me."

"I don't trust *you.*"

"Just a dance."

"What for?"

"Because we agreed."

Jill looked toward the bar. Did she see herself and Raymond? Did she see the two men now sitting at the bar? After a moment she stood up, taking Raymond's extended hand. He led her to the dance floor, placed his arm around her waist, and began slow dancing. He could feel the tension in her back, the stiffness in her legs as she involuntarily followed him.

"You lead," he said.

She stopped for a moment and almost smiled. But she showed no hesitation at trying this new way to dance. In a moment they were moving around the floor, but in a reverse mirror image of how they'd danced only seconds earlier.

All of a sudden Raymond was no longer dancing with Jill. He was instead chasing her down the stairs that led to the beach. She was ahead of him, running for the south point. The tide was high, water lapping at the bottom step. He carefully picked his way on the stairs until he hit sand, which had a sudden spring to it because of a piece of driftwood that lay at the bottom.

Raymond lost his balance as a result of stepping on the jetsam. He fell into the shallow, cold sea. His shoes immediately filled with gritty wetness, his legs becoming as heavy as cement posts. The wave that hit the steps pulled back with the tidal surge, colliding with a new incoming wave, which made a loud clap and shot a geyser-like line of spray along the shore as far as he could see. He pushed himself to his feet.

The wet sand before him glowed in the stark light from above. Now almost at the south point he saw the lightest movement from a dark form. He knew the form was a wife, a woman, a person.

Running toward the form and feeling lightheaded, he felt Jill's grip tighten on his hand, felt her pull him hard into her body, felt her pelvis bump against his own as he went the wrong way on the dance floor. As he began relaxing, he heard the sudden and distinct cacophony of sounds around him. The restaurant curtains flapping in the steady night breeze. The bass guitar, lead guitar, snare drums, even the words the singer told. But loudest of all he heard the unseen and truculent ocean scraping the beach, always scraping the beach.

My Grand-
father's Eye

R ey stepped back, focusing on his grandfather's pink
left eye, which appeared to be turning itself inside out.

"Father Miller won't write me a letter."

"What are you talking about?"

Juan had once been tall but now was shorter than
Rey. Rey himself wasn't short, but he'd always remembered Juan towering above him. Although Juan sometimes claimed over one hundred years as his age—nobody
in the family knew his actual birth year because he gave
differing birth dates depending upon who asked—he easily kept up with Rey on walks to the lake. Even in the heat
of the Elsinore afternoon, he wore old gabardine slacks
and a flannel shirt with a wool stocking cap over his head.

"A letter to keep me out of the draft."

"It's not up to Father Miller."

Juan, when in his teens, had crossed over the Mexican
border and filtered south, all the way to the state of Mor-
elos, where he'd joined Zapata's troops. The family didn't

claim Mexico as their homeland; New Mexico held that particular status. But Juan had believed in the revolutions, though it took another war, this time in Europe, for him to forsake this particular folly. And it had been in Spain where Juan deserted the Catholic Church.

"I don't want to go. I don't want to end up like Rudy." Rey hurt deep in his heart having said this.

"Don't go, then."

"Shit," Rey muttered.

Juan turned back to his sketch. "Can you see the lines already in the painting? I'm putting them in charcoal so they will become constant."

Rey looked at the whitewashed section of wall. It was a large area, and Rey'd not seen his grandfather sketch directly upon a wall before. The brush marks ended in a randomness that bothered him. But in the interior of the whitewashed area he saw amphibian ghosts circling a shiny box that was on a chair. A strange bird with three wings was on the far left of the charcoal drawing, hovering next to a female ghost with long flowing hair.

"Yes," Rey lied.

"No, you don't." Juan stepped back from the drawing and looked at his work. "Now, what's all this tragedy?"

The studio was small, cramped, and completely full of painting utensils: turpentine; shiny number-10 cans holding brushes with the bristle ends up; two stools that served as palettes, separate universes of color; old, clunky easels that held paintings in various stages of completion. High up, a clerestory window covered in dust let in fading light. A stone fireplace, once white, was now covered in black all over the front, scarred from winter fires. Ashes swirled forward in small puffs, as if the fireplace itself were alive and breathing.

"I'm in trouble."

Juan sighed. "Let's go out on the swing and enjoy the evening."

In the living room hens were settling in for the night, roosting on a couch, on a chair, on a chest of drawers, on a flat painting.

Damn, Rey muttered so that Juan wouldn't hear. He hated the fact that chickens lived in the house. He knew this wasn't the way you were supposed to live. None of his friends' families behaved in this way.

But then, Rey no longer seemed to have friends. David, his best friend, had enlisted the summer after high school. He'd *wanted* to go to Vietnam but, as luck would have it, wasn't able to. He was sent to Korea. And there, while on sentry duty at night, he was shot by a sniper. Hector and Joe were doing time for holding up a gas station with a rifle. The entire affair was a misunderstanding; the rifle was an unloaded pellet gun, and Hector and Joe had been drunk, acting on a stupid dare. But there you have it, they were at Terminal Island, doing hard time. They didn't have to face the draft.

Billy was run down on graduation night by a hit-and-run driver. And Rudy, his brother, his closest friend, what could you say about that?

A movement from the surrounding trees made Rey shiver. The giant jacarandas wiggled. It wasn't quite dark.

"*Sientate, mi'jo,*" Juan said, motioning to the old swing. Rey sat on the frond-strewn cushions he'd sat on so many times before with his grandfather. But the dogs were gone. The Chihuahuas used to jump on Rey, sleep in his lap, growl with jealousy at each other. Juan hadn't replaced them as one by one they were stolen or hit by cars.

"What's that?" Rey asked, pointing to a lump on the patio.

"My opossum." Again Juan gave out a sigh, this time a huge one. The possum looked like a dead rat in the darkening light.

"Is it dead?"

"Yes."

"Where's your shovel?"

"What for?"

Rey stood up from the swing and moved toward the dead animal. "I'll throw it in the bushes." He scooted it away from the swing.

"It'll stink."

"I'll throw it across the street."

"It'll still stink."

"Let's cremate him."

"No!" Juan said.

He walked to Rey, bent down, and scooped up the baby marsupial with his large, bony hands, and Rey saw his grandfather's long fingernails, brittle with age, saw the big splotches of discolored skin contrasting with the thin fur of the possum. Rey backed up in fear of smelling something horrible.

"We'll bury it. I have a spot picked out." At the back of the house the wind hit them full force "When I die, I want you to bury me on the property."

"You're not dying, Pa."

They walked behind the weathered picket fence.

"I want you to wrap me in wet sheets."

Sure, everyone died. Rudy had died too, and Rey knew his grandfather would someday pass on, but death was the one thing Rey had thought about far too much lately.

"You'll have to soak the sheets overnight so I don't dry out."

"Stop it, Pa."

"Feel the *viento*?"

Rey's lips were cracked and dry, but the air was alive with electricity from the out-of-control wind. "You'll outlive us all."

Jacaranda fronds fell wholesale to the ground. Under the vine-covered carport Rey found a shovel. The handle was worn smooth, and it felt slick, almost wet, in his hands as he began uncovering dirt.

The ground was hard and dry and the loose dirt swirled, making Rey squint, making him push back wisps of hair that escaped from his ponytail.

"Another foot," Juan whispered. He placed the possum on the ground. "I'll be right back."

Rey leaned against the battered carport that housed the even more battered Volkswagen. He closed his eyes, letting moisture soothe his mounting headache. Nearly all last night he'd been unable to sleep. Thinking about his course of action. Or inaction. He knew the priest had been a last resort. A letter wouldn't have helped anyway.

While once again digging, he thought of Canada. Resistors went up north. Sweden was too far, Canada just right. Plus, they welcomed you. The end of the shovel hit a large, smooth river rock. He knelt to remove it.

As he dug deeper, he wondered why Rudy's body had never been found. Why they had that stupid memorial service that didn't satisfy anyone. And why the military had taken no responsibility. There had been no burial. Maybe that was the problem. No body. No Rudy.

Juan returned with a pail. "I'll show you how it's done. That's enough! The hole is big enough to put me in."

It wasn't that large, but without paying attention, Rey had made the grave too deep.

"You set the sheets on the ground like this," Juan said, placing small cut lengths on the ground. He put the possum on the longest one. Then he wrapped it over and over. The blowing dust didn't seem to bother Juan. "Mine will be much larger and you'll have to soak them in the bathtub.

"Stop it!" Rey said, pushing strands of hair out of his face.

"You might need help. I asked Eddie across the way if you can't do it alone."

"I'm not burying you like this."

"Why not? I want to be close to the paintings."

Those fucking paintings. "You're not dying." Rey turned and looked down to the lake. It was a dark rippled apparition, whitecaps whipped in the center. Next to him, Juan had created a tiny mummy, which he poured water over.

The problem with all the talk of burials was that the old man was serious. The older he became, the more disdain he held for convention. Rey knew there was little possibility of burying his grandfather in this way. Besides, Juan wasn't a marsupial.

When they finished, the night was dark black. One of those moonless, lightless Lake Elsinore nights. The air was hot and dry and the wind swirled uncontrollably.

The dream was ocean. And in the dream Rey's head burned. But the sea was cool and it soothed him. A shiny piece of metal was in a crevice. In water. Everything was fluid, slow motion, but Rey couldn't get to the metal, and it seemed that faces were watching him through the water. And sounds. Music, muffled by liquid. Louder. Clearer. It was radio music? No, children laughing.

When he awoke to the strange sounds, it was still dark. He heard voices in song, but they were faraway voices. The sounds faded, yet they were still slightly audible.

Groggy, he found himself at the doorway to his grandfather's studio. Inside, Juan sketched more figures on the wall. The three-winged bird now had two heads, one at each end of its body. The long-haired ghost woman smiled, her almond-shaped eyes squinting, her legs spread obscenely in flight. A salamander/dog ghost clawed escape from the scene. Rey wondered if his grandfather was the source of the sounds.

"Pa, did you hear the sounds?"

"What are you doing awake?

"I heard sounds."

"What kind of sounds?"

"Like music."

"I heard nothing."

"Tell me about it."

"It's nothing."

"Does it come from you?"

"No."

"Where does it come from?"

"It's not important."

"Do you hear the same thing I hear?"

"I already told you, forget it. It's nothing. Go back to sleep."
Juan turned to his sketch.

Quietly, Rey walked outside to relieve himself. A full-blown
windstorm tried to displace everything surrounding the house. He
squinted to shield his eyes, and his hair blew in a wild mess. He
closed his eyes while pissing and then opened them. The Big Dip-
per and the North Star beckoned him through the dust.

In the morning Rey was awakened by the sound of a crash. He
stood up, still dressed in yesterday's clothes, and looked out the
window. The birdbath had fallen. In the center of the birdbath
Juan had placed a plaster statue of Saint Christopher. Saint Christopher had held up one hand in greeting, in peace, but Rey now saw
the arm broken and lying on the ground.

Outside, the wind tried to push the jacarandas off their axes.
Junipers on the other side of the street bounced to three o'clock,
heading west, then popped back up to twelve o'clock. The dust
pushing through the air made his eyes feel gritty once again.

Placing the birdfeeder upright and leaning it against a dwarf
walnut tree so that it wouldn't fall, Rey closed his eyes and felt the
energy of the wind. He picked up the statue and the broken arm.

Saint Christopher had sort of been banned by the Catholic
Church. Where formerly he had been the patron saint of travelers,
he was now just a regular saint. Or was he still a saint? Rey couldn't
remember, though he knew there had been some change in status
for Saint Christopher.

Back inside the house he shook his hair up and down to rid
himself of the dust. Without thinking, he placed the saint on a
pedestal that was attached to the wall. The pedestal was a flower

cut in half, a bloom with a flat top that seemed perfect for holding Saint Christopher. All the colors on the saint had long since weathered, so that the robe and the hair were a pink plaster color. Feeling like the fallen saint, he placed its small arm in his pocket.

At the studio door he saw Juan asleep in the fetal position on the discolored old couch. His grandfather had covered himself with a newspaper. Rey knew the old man slept in snatches, rising during the night and painting, and then sleeping for hours during the day, and then rising, doing some chore, and then sleeping once again.

"Good-bye, Pa," Rey whispered.

Once inside the car, he tied the arm of Saint Christopher to the rearview mirror. He didn't know which way to go, though he almost felt like driving to the huge induction center on Spring Street in Los Angeles and telling them he'd made a mistake—he'd forgotten the date of his induction physical, could he take it now, please? Yet the die was cast, the future set.

Straight ahead, he saw the outline of the Ortega Mountains in silhouette. The early morning glare off the lake was blinding, and whitecaps frothed in the angry water. Not knowing which way to go, Rey slowly pulled away from the house, watching the dangling arm of Saint Christopher, thinking how it was pink, like his grandfather's eye, and knowing, too, that the next move was already made.

Work: Number One (Love)

B utch claims to be born again but really isn't, not in a strict sense. He drinks beer and smokes. Oh, sure, he believes, he just doesn't live the word of the Lord the way the other guys say they do. Brian, a decent carpenter on the job, is truly born again, is the purest human being you'll ever meet, and has transcended all the worldly bullshit.

Your goal is to be the hottest apprentice in Orange County. And you're close. You're in demand. Guys want you working for them because you'll make them money, pure and simple. The shit you know you pump it out. The stuff you don't know, and there's a lot, comes quickly with good teachers. You're looking for the hottest carpenters around to work with. Pick their brains, learn their tricks, learn their shortcuts, learn what's acceptable versus what isn't. Attitude is everything. Why you got away from tract work. Guys with bad attitudes there, guys who're so insecure it's palpable.

The reason you're working with this small Christian

framing company building custom homes. The best apprentice-
ship in the world. Their boy was a carpenter; you don't work for
yourself, you work for the Lord.

Butch is from Colorado, down on his luck, and he worked with
Cal and Dan, the owners of the company, years ago. They took him
on, no questions asked. Butch lives in his camper shell on the job,
without his wife, who is still back home. He's midthirties, as are
Dan and Cal, sort of old for framers, but you're midtwenties, sort of
old for an apprentice. You've got a college degree to show for the
missing years. Cal and Dan have a successful framing company.
Butch has a truck.

You were in love but have recently broken up. Actually been
left. Serena was beautiful, no doubt about it. This good-looking:
Once when she was walking along the Coast Highway in Laguna, a
guy goo-gooing her while driving rear-ended another car. Serena
looks so good in Levi's. That's why the guy was ogling. That's what
caused a wreck. And you were hooked on sex with her. At that time
you thought it was love but it wasn't. It was pussy addiction. Addiction to the body. The ass that caused the accident. What you
were addicted to.

Now you cry on the way to work. And a lot at home. But during the day you're building four custom homes that are models for
the tract that will come later. You're running circles around the
other apprentices. So much so that Cal lets you piece ceiling joist
on all the units. Then he teaches you how to cut stairs. Next he'll
teach you how to cut roofs, but Jeff, one of the guys who goes to
church with them, complains, saying he's not learning anything
new.

So you are told to stack the roofs with Butch. Stacking means
building the roof structure after the rafters are cut. All four houses
are stacked conventionally, which means the rafters are custom
cut. The garages stack with prefab trusses. You and Butch work well
together, you're on a roll, flyin', jammin'. Kickin' ass. The first

morning Jeff stacks. After he and Cal cut all the roofs, he falls. He's not got the body for high work—where the money is. He's pear shaped and tentative, and his legs are too bulky, and he looks scared most of the time. From that morning on, you get to work with either Cal or Dan, whoever is doing the most complex job. You'll learn how to build a house from the ground up, the reason you got into building in the first place.

After the models are framed, there's a lull in the work. Dan and Cal have some huge custom homes coming up, but there are two, three weeks in between. They'll let you come into the office, learn about lumber take-offs and bidding, but you're twenty-five and it's summer and you don't want to be inside, though that's where the serious money is. The problem is this: All you can think of is Serena. Her smell, her voice, her body, the things she wore and the things she did for you. You know you can't concentrate if you're not moving. You and Butch will partner up. Keep moving.

You started on the tracts clearing scraps from framed houses. That meant you salvaged any wood that was long enough to make into fire blocking, anything 14½ inches or better. On the job they called you the Indian because your long black hair was tied in a ponytail and you wore a bandanna as a sweatband. They were the disco years, and your look was iconoclastic, if not downright out of it.

Gathering scrap was so boring you made a contest of it with yourself. How fast could you clear a house of temporaries and block? By the end of the first week you were fucken *running* you were so bored. They got you right on the cutoff saw, a far superior job than mindlessly gathering wood. Same thing with the cutoff saw—you competed with yourself to do the job faster each day. A day's lumber in six hours, in five hours, in half a day.

Then you built loads. One afternoon the bone driver gave you an order for his house, a small load. He'd take it after quitting time, he told you confidentially. You said nothing to him, continuing to build legitimate loads till quitting time. When the bone driver questioned you as to why you'd not done his request, you told him to build his own fucken load, you weren't his thief. Somehow this got back to the foreman, who gave you a job away from the bone driver installing shear paneling, another step up. One dollar a sheet. Four-foot by eight-foot plywood. You flew, putting up eighty, then ninety, then one hundred twenty sheets in a day. But it wore you down, even at twenty-four years old.

Now you and Butch drive around until you get on with a framing foreman who knows you. Framing walls. It's slow at first, until you learn the houses, and then you guys start making some money. You've arrived—a journeyman carpenter is splitting the take fifty-five forty-five, the best deal you've gotten so far, as close to equal as you can get without being equal.

The days are hot and long. You frame a house and a half per day. Butch is saving all his money. He's leaving for Colorado next week to bring back his wife. You've got nothing going, so you work long hours. No dates, no love, no social life. You're wounded, wanting to be with Serena so badly it's all you think about, but she's gone.

The entire week all Butch talks about is how smart his wife is. How talented. How beautiful. Friday morning Butch is pumped. And stupid. He can't concentrate. You frame your house before lunch and tell Butch to take off. You'll nail top plate and detail the next house so it's ready for Monday.

Really? Butch says in his high-pitched "fun" voice. He's got ocean blue eyes and blond crew-cut hair, and he wears old double-knit pants with waffle stompers. He's a nice guy. You want to see him happy.

Go, you say.

It's funny how you get attached to a guy when you sweat and work together. Especially when you partner up. Especially in such a competitive environment as piece-working on the tract. You and

Butch are respected. It's quiet without him. He's in love. You're in pain. He'll be back Monday morning.

Seven a.m. Monday morning, no Butch. So you start working. Framing walls alone. Your partner has left you. Oh, shit.

Finally, around ten, you see Butch's pickup drive onto the tract. It's loaded down with household goods, a box-spring mattress leering from the very top. His camper shell and cab are full of things as well, so you can barely see two humans occupying the truck.

You're framing second-story walls, called tops. Walls are lying all over the floor because you can't raise them yourself. All the perimeter walls are framed, braces cut in, and a few interior walls, the smaller ones, framed and stacked on top of others.

We went out for breakfast this morning, Butch says, a shit-eating grin on his face. The look of a happy man. The grin of a fulfilled man.

The rest of the morning you stand walls. By the time the roach coach honks for lunch, you've almost knocked out the house. Butch can barely contain himself he's so excited to have Corinne here with him.

Usually you and Butch eat together, sometimes with other framers. Today is sort of awkward because not only does he have his wife with him, but he's not said anything about the morning. About adjusting the cut. He's focused only on Corinne.

At the catering truck where you get your cold drinks the guys are commenting on how it doesn't look good to have your wife on the job, all your possessions in your truck. As if Butch's condition is contagious or something.

On your way to your van where your lunch is, Butch says, Come over here, I want to introduce you to someone special.

The tailgate is down on Butch's truck. Corinne, his wife, is sitting on it. She's large boned and overweight and large breasted and wearing Levi's cutoffs that show her big legs. Her hair is long and up in a bun. Her fingernails are long and blood red. She's got on a lot of makeup, even in the heat. She's smoking a cigarette and drinking from a quart bottle of Pepsi.

This here's my partner, Butch says to Corinne. To me he says, Ain't she purty?

Corinne's swirling feet make small clouds of dust in the powdery dirt, and you can just make out her pink-painted toenails, and you know Serena was right, you didn't love her, not like this.

The Wind Blows It Away

As Gil approaches the freeway off-ramp, he is suddenly overcome by a strange feeling. Traffic comes to a halt. He is in the number-three lane, surrounded by cars and pickup trucks and motor homes and cars pulling boats and a few big rigs, though not many, for it is Saturday afternoon. On the freeway with him are all the accoutrements of the "sexy" southern California outdoor lifestyle, life as a television commercial for adult toys: Two lanes over some guys have dirt bikes lashed in the bed of their pickup truck. One lane over and a number of cars ahead of him, another load of guys has a Jet Ski on a trailer behind their Suburban. A van in front of Gil has bicycles strapped to a roof rack, and one of the tires slowly spins in the breeze. There is only one beat-up car stopped on the freeway with Gil and the other travelers; it is an old nondescript American car and it has in it what looks like two families of beachgoers. They are dark people, working people, Gil thinks, and he is glad they, too, can go to the beach and enjoy the end of summer even though they don't have the requisite $10,000 worth of accompanying gear. It doesn't really matter how much fun gear you have, for if the freeway comes to a standstill, you're stuck in traffic just like every other chump on the road.

The strange feeling continues to buzz deep in Gil's gut, something he can't put his finger on, something akin to having taken a drug and then waiting for its effects to hit you. Something that says, Relax, you're on for the duration whether you like it or not.

After a time of sitting on the freeway, going nowhere, surrounded by other vehicles with their engines idling, Gil turns his ignition off and gets out of his car. He walks around it, as if this will somehow break the spell that holds everyone in stasis, but nothing happens; the cars and all the people remain where they are.

He looks around the parking lot of cars, hoping that he knows someone, though it seems as if everyone from Gil's former life has been blown away by a strong wind. He becomes very bold, "changing lanes," walking up to a car with what looks like friendly people in it. They are a couple on the cusp of middle age, probably out for a weekend jaunt. As he approaches the driver, he sees the window go up. The man won't look at Gil as he stands looking down. One of the things you're to do to discourage "road rage" is not look your potential assailant in the eye. Gil isn't an assailant, however.

"Have you heard what's going on?" he says to the man behind the auto glass.

No answer.

Gil moves on.

He next stops to talk with a bunch of guys in a lowered dually pulling a racing boat. The dually is all black, the boat white with red racing stripes. He catches a glimpse of one of the guys in the extended cab snorting cocaine.

"What's up?" he says to the guy riding shotgun.

"Dead in the water," the guy says. He's huge, his arms as big as Gil's legs. "Anybody tell you anything?"

"People are afraid to talk," Gil says. "Afraid of their fucking shadows."

The guy smiles. He takes a drink from his beer. "People are fucked."

The guy is right, Gil knows. You can't even talk to people any longer.

Suddenly a few cars far ahead lurch forward. Gil hustles back to his small truck, starts the engine with the expectation of actually going forward on the fucking freeway, but no dice.

He turns on the radio in the hopes of hearing a traffic report that will tell him the exact cause of the freeway shutdown. He presses the buttons on his radio's tuner to no avail, getting only talk shows and football games. Finally he tunes in to a traffic report that is just ending, though nothing is said about the freeway shutdown. As is often the case, most of the traffic reports concern only Los Angeles motorists, not those in Orange County.

So Gil sits in the stopped traffic, listening to a USC football game, waiting. Waiting is something he's good at, he feels, for it seems that most of his life is spent waiting. Waiting for his life to take a turn for the better. Waiting to make some big money. Waiting for his father to get better so that he can return home. Waiting for his mother to get stronger so that she can care for his father and bring him home. Waiting for the right woman. As he listens to the football game, he remembers going to the Coliseum all those years ago with his father. SC played Notre Dame. SC was rated number one in the polls. Notre Dame was in the top five. SC had the best running back in the nation at the time, O. J. Simpson. Notre Dame held Simpson at bay the entire game. They just keyed on him, stopping him after small gains. Until finally in the third quarter he broke free from the tacklers and scored a touchdown. It was sheer stubborn will that won the game for USC that afternoon. It was a good game, a defensive struggle. After he thinks of the word struggle, Gil can't help thinking of Nicole, and then Ron, and then Justin and Sydney, and then the Goldmans and the Browns and the Simpsons and the Fuhrmans et al., so he changes the station.

He hopes the strange feeling will leave him but it doesn't. He feels dread and excitement at the same time. As he listens to the car show on a talk show station, a reporter breaks in with the "evolving story" affecting Gil. There was a hostage situation that closed down the freeway. A disgruntled somebody or other held a cabby hostage using a hairbrush as a gun. The cabby couldn't see that the "gun" was a hairbrush. He drove his cab until it ran out of gas on the freeway. It is now over and traffic will resume moving shortly, the reporter says.

It's Saturday afternoon and Gil is supposed to go to the convalescent hospital to see his father, then go spend the early evening with his mother, probably taking her out to dinner, and then go with her to see his father in the evening.

It's a great distance from his condominium to his familial home in Seal Beach, where he grew up and where his ailing parents still live. If nothing else, Gilbert is loyal. Every weekend he visits his parents. His mother at home, his father at the convalescent hospital where he now lives. Gil's mother is no longer able to care for his father, who has survived many life-threatening health crises: open heart surgery, triple bypass, strokes, seizures, hip replacement surgery, gall bladder removal. It's like this, the doctor explained to Gilbert after one of the episodes. Your father's like an old car. It still wants to run, it will run, yet all the peripheral parts are breaking. And you have to replace them. Do you understand? We can fix the ailing part but there will be a consequence. Many times it will affect another organ, the operation or procedure will, the doctor explained to Gilbert. He understood all too well.

He knows his father is tired of being paralyzed, tired of being dependent upon his wife to take him to the bathroom, to take him out, to put him in the living room. Gil's father is paralyzed on his left side. He's unable to get out of bed on his own. He's confined to a wheelchair and can no longer speak in complete sentences, except once in a while when he utters some profound, complex thought in a cogent and articulate manner. That's what really gets to Gil. The fact that much of his father's mind is still there but he can't verbalize his needs. Sometimes no means yes. And the opposite. It's tough; everything about his father now boils down to urination and defecation, really. Yet his father and mother are still too much entangled, still have too much physical love between them for his mother to cut loose his father. His father isn't afraid to die; they talked about it. He is fearful of leaving his wife a widow, of leaving Gilbert fatherless. Gil's parents have been married fifty-six years. Gil's marriage lasted a little over one year.

He was with Ceci—living together, that is—for two years prior to the wedding. Gil wanted a small and elegant wedding. Ceci agreed with him. But then her mother took over, throwing an incredibly lavish wedding, the wedding she had always wanted but didn't get. The marriage counselor Gil and Ceci went to said that the marriage was doomed from the start—they weren't honest with each other about what kind of wedding they wanted. He resented being put in the "dishonest" category because he'd been perfectly honest. He wanted a small wedding. In good taste. Just a few friends. Ceci ended up having seven bridesmaids, while Gil had trouble finding seven "friends" who could participate in the ceremony. Over five hundred people attended Gil and Ceci's wedding. Gil's own parents were seated way off on the tennis courts, far removed from the "center" of the wedding, the table where Ceci's parents held court.

When the traffic begins moving slowly forward, Gil remains on the freeway in the knot of cars heading south. His off-ramp is barricaded by police vehicles, and up off the freeway he can see a lone cab surrounded by SWAT team members.

Just before Huntington Beach traffic slows once again. And then it stops. This time Gil sees the cause of the freeway's blockage: a tractor-truck trailer combo has hit a sports car. The small black car is stuck under the wheels of the big rig. People are out of their cars once again. Police cars are at the scene, and others are arriving, and the shrill whoops of ambulances slowly working their way through gridlock come from all directions at once. This time Gil becomes claustrophobic, surrounded by big rigs and other trucks. He can't understand why so many work vehicles are on the road on a weekend. To relax he rolls down his window the way his own father did long ago when he, too, stopped in traffic. The difference being that Gil's father's traffic usually was that of surface streets, not the kind of serious traffic Gil encounters on the region's freeways.

As more and more emergency vehicles appear, the radio finally reports the accident. What the radio reporter says, though, differs from Gil's take on the incident. All he sees is a standard bad accident. The radio report says that indeed there has been a collision between a big rig and an automobile, but further states that there was a shooting after the accident. The motorist whose car was stuck under the truck's wheels this very moment shot the truck driver for scrunching his Ferrari.

Soon the medi-vac appears, landing right on the freeway. Medical personnel tend to the fallen body, loading it into the helicopter, which lifts off like a slow, fat bird.

The sun is going down in the west, which is in Gil's rearview mirror, a glowing ball of orange, and he now wishes he could get off the freeway, get to his parents. But he can't; he's fixed on this roadway, heading south, a victim of the capricious violent times.

He wasn't able to get off at his normal exit. Now he is in such a furious mix of cars he knows that when everyone begins moving again it will take him miles just to change a lane. Nobody will let you in their spot, and everyone will drive at the same rate, and if you want to get a space in another lane you'll have to take it, like surfing. Your ability got you the position on the wave that you deserved.

Gil tunes in another football game. It's the third quarter of the

Super Bowl, Green Bay and the Patriots. Green Bay's ahead. He thinks it strange that they are now replaying games that have already been decided. Where's the tension in that? The game must have been played a few years back, he thinks, though he can't remember the two teams ever having played, yet that isn't unusual, for you forget the big game the second it's over, don't you?

Cars begin slowly moving once again, and again Gil doesn't exit the freeway and turn around, for now in the other direction, north, the direction toward his familial home, traffic is at a standstill. As he drives away from the scene of the shooting—people stop for a number of seconds right on the actual spot, smelling blood and injury, Gil assumes—he can see the reason that the northbound traffic is stopped. A motorcyclist lies on the ground in the gathering dusk, his cycle battered and broken, spewed across lanes like a child's plaything.

Gilbert crawls forward in the slow-moving mass of vehicles, his lights on. He now has a plan. He'll take the Corona del Mar Freeway to Coast Highway and then circle back to Seal Beach in that manner. It's a route that he took many times as an adolescent when he had his own motorcycle, the Scrambler. It was really a dirt bike, but his was street legal, and he remembers the time his wiring went kaput in Newport Beach at night and he had to ride the bike all the way home without headlights or brake lights. But he did it, and now he can do a similar trek back.

When he hits Pacific Coast Highway at MacArthur, Gil doesn't head north. He goes south once again because the lanes north are blocked for street repair. Since he's in the area and the universe is telling him so, he thinks, what the hell, maybe Ceci's at her parents' or something. He can stop by and say hello, if he sees her car out in front of her parents' house. See how she's doing. She's remarried now, he knows. After their separation and divorce, they remained on pretty good terms. They even "dated" a few times, the euphemism for having sex, which Gil found depressing and pathetic, since they were still married. It made him furious, having to date his wife just so he could get laid. But Ceci was cool in that regard; she didn't withhold sex from him ever. So that's Gil's coalescing plan. See if he can talk Ceci into cheating on her new husband. Why not? What the fuck does he care if he ruins her new marriage? He doesn't. In fact, when he thinks in this way, it makes him almost happy. Not true happiness. Maybe revenge is a better word, though the guy she married wasn't responsible for their breakup, or so Ceci claimed. He still wonders if Ceci cheated on him. He couldn't ask her because he himself was guilty of cheating on her.

. Before Gil's marriage to Ceci he dated a woman who lived with another woman in a condo. The other woman dated a guy who got married. Yet he still came over, even after he was married, and had sex with the roommate. And this went on for years. Maybe Gil could reach some sort of similar agreement with Ceci. After Ceci left him she was truly cool about coming over and having sex with him every week. Then her visits occurred less frequently. And then she only called. And then she stopped calling. Gil never once called her.

After turning left onto Coast Highway, he turns right onto Carnation, heads down past the park, crosses Bayside, and then drives along the cliff overlooking Big Corona. He tries not to think of his father, staring at the ceiling, listening to the various screamers and moaners and hackers and coughers who also live at the convalescent hospital. He tries not to think of his mother, alone and waiting and needy, coveting human contact, preferably female, but Gilbert will do nicely in a pinch, which he does every weekend. He parks his car on the beach side of Cliff Drive, right across the street from Ceci's parents' house.

It's a large two-story structure and looks like the Taco Bell mansion. Ceci's parents didn't always have money, and it showed in the design of the house they built overlooking the ocean. Ceci's father is an inventor. (You don't think of inventors when you think of Chicanos, but think Thomas Alva Edison. Alva was Edison's

Mexican mother's name.) Ceci's father invented some sort of egg carton and made a bundle. He invented some other stuff as well, though nothing as important as the egg carton. At one time Ceci's parents were working class, just like Gil's parents.

Thus the vulgar wedding. And the reason Gil was allowed into Ceci's life in the first place. Her father and mother both liked Gil quite a bit, even though they wanted their daughter to marry "up." But that probably would have meant Ceci marrying a *gabacho,* so they accepted Gilbert finally.

It's an oddly cold evening, one with almost no strollers about, and those who are walking wear long parkas, and one woman even has a muffler, which the wind buffets. Gil isn't prepared for how cold it is outside his car.

He finds it odd that the houses along the cliff seldom have people in them. Usually they are left in some sort of *Architectural Digest* photo mode: the draperies back, the chandelier lighted, the table set, but no humans around. This is the case with Ceci's house. It looks as if every light in the house is on, even the one upstairs where Ceci's old bedroom is. Maybe she's home. Maybe her new marriage went bad, the way theirs had. What the hell, he thinks, I'll knock on the door.

The doorbell is some sort of chime apparatus, something that he always found extremely irritating and slow. The help has instructions from Ceci's mother *not* to answer the door until the chime stops. While the chime dawdles, he looks at all the color on the front porch. Bougainvillea, daisies, alyssum, carnations, and roses.

The maid answers the door. He knows her, though he can't remember her name. She lives in the small guest house in back with her husband, who cares for the property. She seems to recognize him but doesn't remember his name either, or simply doesn't wish to acknowledge him. She smiles. "Everyone's in the Bahamas. On a cruise. Cecelia is with her husband."

She has to throw that tidbit out, he thinks. "I'm her husband. We were married in the Church."

He won't be able to say this much longer because Ceci's father is paying for an annulment of their marriage. They want him to say that he was a fuckup, that he had no intention of remaining married. It's probably true.

"They'll be back next month," she says. She closes the door with Gil still wanting to talk.

He hoped he could get inside Ceci's house, but he's now outside where it's suddenly dark and empty and echoing wind sounds permeate the street. The wind's cooking over the ocean, the waves crashing on shore, an eerie out-of-season winter postcard. Is it cold enough to snow? he wonders. He doesn't think he should walk in the freakish winter air, but another force tells him that he should, so he begins walking along the sidewalk that leads to Little Corona.

He shivers as he walks, and he ponders, What is it all for? To die alone in a convalescent home, cared for and touched by paid strangers. He makes his way to the park bench at the top of Little Corona, where he sits on the bench, shivering big time. And hoping that he won't cry.

Gil thinks of other times when he sat at this very same bench with Ceci, nights when a pianist serenaded promenading lovers, and now he can only snicker at such memories. How hokey can you get, for God's sake? A pianist playing a portable keyboard at dusk so that lovers can become intimate? Romantic? It's like the mariachis at a Mexican restaurant or a violinist at an Italian restaurant. Or a trio at the jazz club. If you tip the minstrel, he might show you some favoritism, might linger at your table, which might bode well for you later, should you get lucky, should you get in the "zone." Gilbert thinks these things and knows he's jaded.

As he's sitting there, a woman materializes through the dark and swollen air. She sits on the other end of the bench, fidgeting with her parka. Removing the hood or something. He feels the woman's presence, an animal, primal vibration. Something deeply imprinted in his psyche, something he is unable to control. Man/woman. The birds and the bees. He smells her perfume, something like Opiate or Opium, something Ceci herself wears. A big moon hangs in the gray night sky, obscuring Mars or Saturn; he can never remember which planet is visible in the early evening sky. It's winter—no people, no cars, a cold silvery moon, and a huge west swell, the swell of winter.

After a time the woman says, "How are you?"

"Terrible, but I'm used to it." She chuckles. The woman is pretty large, he sees even in the dark, but other than that he has not a clue as to what she looks like or who she is.

"Who do you think controls the world? Men or women?"

Her voice is husky, not in the least bit weak, he thinks. She is not a weak person, he thinks, not if she sits on a park bench at night, initiating conversation with a stranger. And she isn't very old if she is pondering sophomoric questions such as the one she asked, he figures. He also tries to remember the line he read in a novel, the title or writer he can't remember, which goes, Women control 70 percent of the world's wealth and 100 percent of the pussy. "Women, obviously," Gil says.

"I don't think so," she says. "Why?"

"Because they coexist with a physically superior counterpart," Gil says. "Sort of like 'man' in the jungle. Man is not the strongest animal, yet by virtue of his reason, he can coexist and in fact dominate his surroundings."

"Women don't dominate their worlds," the woman says.

"Sometimes they do." Gil thinks of the power Ceci has over him, the power his mother has over his father.

"Why has there never been a woman president, then?"

Please, Gil thinks. He wants to ask her if she prefers to give head or receive it, but he refrains. Of course, he thinks, this is the very thing she refers to. "Wait, there will be. And sooner than you think."

"Where does that path lead?" she asks, motioning to the cut in the foliage in front of the bench.

"A lookout point."

"Do you want to show it to me?"

"You bet," Gil says.

"I just got off work," she says, standing up. "At Swenson's."

"Oh." He sees that his analogy about women existing as the weaker sex breaks down in the presence of this woman. She is larger than Gil. Could probably bench-press him, in fact. And he isn't small.

As if sensing his thoughts, the woman says, "I'm on a volleyball scholarship at UC."

"Okay." He's uphill from her, and still she is taller. "I'm just hanging out. I used to live around here." Not entirely true, so he adds, "I know someone who lives across the street."

"Ah," the woman says.

"C'mon, then. I'll show you the lookout. It's a good place to watch sunsets."

They begin walking down the steep trail that winds its way through the manzanita bushes and the shrubbery that hug the cliffside. With the onshore breeze, a slight fog blows in, which really highlights the big moon. He waits for the woman at various turns in the path. At one particularly steep part, he takes hold of her hand, guiding her over a break in the pathway.

"You really do know this place," she says, letting go of his hand.

"I've got friends living here."

The foghorn begins its lonely wail. And every so often he can hear tires making the turn up on the slick pavement above them. When Gil gets to the perch he stops, putting out his arm so the woman can go no farther. There is a steep drop down onto rocks, which are plastered with the breaking surf.

"Be careful."

"Whoa," the woman says. "I would have never found it on my own."

"You might have. It might have taken you some time, but you would have stumbled upon it, no doubt. Not at night, though.

Don't come here until you've walked it yourself in the daylight. Okay?"

They are close, close enough so that Gil can make out the contours of her face. She is very young, he thinks.

They sit down on the dirt, the woman offering part of her parka to him, which she's removed and which he is grateful for. They're shoulder to shoulder.

The surf crashes below them, and it is so noisy and so all encompassing as to render talking difficult. A manzanita bush tickles Gil's neck.

"You can kiss me," the young woman says.

"Is this what you want?"

"It's Saturday night."

"That it is."

"I'm old enough to know what I'm doing," she says. "If that's what you're thinking."

"I wasn't really thinking age." He is trying to imagine not being so angry with Ceci.

The woman puts her arm around Gil and leans her head on his shoulder. They sit there for a time as if they know each other, as if they are lovers. Maybe even friends as well. The tide is rising, and the waves break over the rocks with winter's fury. After a time Gil kisses her on the cheek and then on the ear. He smells her hair, which smells vaguely of sweat and salt air. The woman takes her hair out of its ponytail. Gil still hasn't the vaguest idea what she looks like, nor does he care. He likes this brave woman. Either that or she is extremely foolish. But she is taking a chance in the same way that he is. Both emotionally and physically. He remembers Hemingway's discourse in *Death in the Afternoon,* the one about the dangers of bullfighting, when the bullfighter was bound to perform his manly duty when *not* in the ring. Having sex with the groupies. Syphilis was that era's AIDS. Syphilis led to blindness, dementia, death. Gangster of love. Al Capone.

He touches her neck softly and kisses her forehead and puts his hand under her sweatshirt, cupping her breast over her bra. She kisses him harder, their lips pressed together with a hungry fury. He feels her body and she feels his, and they undress each other just enough in the frigid night air; she even has a condom.

When they are finished the woman says, "I want you to leave."

"Why?"

"I don't wish to know you. I want to listen to the sea."

Gil doesn't know her name, nor does she offer it. When he says good night she doesn't answer, and he can see her staring out over the ocean.

The northbound freeway on-ramp is closed for repairs, so he thinks he'll drive south until the next off-ramp, get off, circle back, and take the freeway north, toward his parents' house. He drives south, and before he realizes it, he's at Laguna Canyon Road, where he tries to exit the freeway. Traffic comes to a standstill. He's met by a highway patrolman who will not let motorists use the off-ramp. "Go south," the patrolman orders as Gil rolls past him. "Police activity. Keep moving."

Traffic is light. Instinctively he turns on his radio. As he drives still farther south, he hears on the radio that there has been a shoot-out on the off-ramp. Heavily armed men in full body armor robbed an all-night market. Police gave chase, and when they blocked the on-ramp, the gunfight ensued. Two robbers dead, three policemen wounded. Police are still searching for accomplices; ergo, various freeway exits will be affected for the rest of the night. This on- and off-ramp will be closed indefinitely, the radio announcer says.

As he drives, a sad, cold rain falls, one that almost looks like snow. It greases the roadway, so that once on a tight curve his tires float in a fishtail. A syrupy slush covers the road, and a few motorists are unable to drive, so they simply pull over on the side of the road, except one, who stops right where the lane line should be, if you could see it, which you can't. He carefully passes the abandoned car.

The light is bad and he can't see much of anything. It's like those white-out conditions when you ski. Sort of light out, too much light, in fact, as you are enveloped in clouds. The slush-like rain obscures the entire world.

After driving a long time, he finds himself on Crown Valley Parkway, the first place that he's able to exit the freeway. It's odd, the way the universe is conspiring to make him head south. Every time he wants to go back north, to head back to his routine, something intrudes. The rain is steadier now and wetter, no longer that slushy stuff he encountered earlier. Soon he's on the Pacific Coast Highway once again, heading south.

Gil once dated a woman named Shannon. Shannon lived with a woman named Michaela. Gil first dated Michaela, but there was no chemistry between them. Somehow or other Gil and Shannon were thrown together, and there was no weirdness over the fact that he'd previously dated Michaela. Gil thinks he might have been in love with Shannon, but she had a thirteen-year-old daughter, and in those days he had specific standards about the criteria for a potential wife. Never married was one of them. No children was another. But he became involved in the lives of Shannon and her daughter, Sydney. Whenever Gil spent the night with Shannon, Sydney would insist on giving him a good-night kiss on the lips. He knew that Syd had to make do without a father, and he tried his best to be friends with her and knew, too, that he couldn't and wouldn't be her father. The kisses on the lips made him uncomfortable. Shannon laughed at them.

Gil was an early riser. One morning when he was up and had showered but before he was dressed (he'd go directly to work from Shannon's), Sydney made a point of barging into the bathroom and getting something she needed. The unsettling part for him was that Sydney wore no clothes, only a bra and panties. She exuded sexuality, and she knew what she was doing, he felt. And he didn't need to get between this mother and daughter. Not that he would have. But he wouldn't allow a flirtation even, for that's what Syd was up to at the least. After that morning Sydney's kisses were even more forceful. At every opportunity she would prance around half clothed. He found himself physically attracted to her, though he would never have acted on it in a million years. So he began a slow withdrawal, which culminated in a story Shannon told him in which she was almost raped and in fact was forced to have oral sex with a guy. It went like this: Shannon was at a party where there was cocaine. So-and-so, who was having the party, had all the cocaine. Shannon loved coke. After the gathering was over, she stuck around the house with the guy she'd just met. She and the guy snorted and hung out.

Except when Shannon was ready to leave, the guy said, You owe me.

Owe you what? Shannon said.

For the coke, he said.

Okay, Shannon said. How much? She fumbled with her purse.

No money, he said.

Shannon thought he was kidding but there was a dark vibe about him, so she made for the door. He grabbed her, throwing her back into the living room, and began groping her body. He squeezed her arm so hard that there were still marks on it when Shannon showed Gil a number of days later. Little off-brown spots on her biceps. The guy undid his pants. Shannon pleaded with him, begged him, cried. Of course, the guy was too whiffed to do anything, so Shannon sucked his limp dick a few swipes until he let her go.

Shannon cried when she recounted the story to Gil.

He felt like shit because his only thought was, What were you doing in a situation like that? Happily, he didn't say anything. He held Shannon, but thought her somewhat responsible for what happened. He felt it was mostly Shannon's fault for whiffing out with a stranger. And something changed for him. There was a distance between them that formerly wasn't there.

One night post rape story Gil called Shannon. Late at night. He needed to talk with her. Michaela answered the phone, telling him that Shannon wasn't around and wouldn't be back until very late. Sydney was staying at a friend's house. Gil needed to talk, needed not to be alone, so he went over and hung out with Michaela. They snorted coke. And drank. When it was very late, he talked Michaela into fucking him. This broke up Shannon and Michaela's friendship. Shannon and Sydney moved out of the house.

He heard that Shannon took a free fall. Sydney went to live with her father. Shannon began doing heroin. And then became a streetwalker to pay for her junk. Slamming heroin and fucking jarheads in San Clemente.

San Clemente's main street is deserted, the road thick and black from the recent rain. One woman who walks the street gives off puffs in front of her as she breathes. Gil cruises by her twice, the second time pulling over to the curb. The woman stops, looking at him with arms akimbo.

"I'm looking for someone," Gil says.

"I don't want to talk," the woman says. "Too cold for talk."

Gil asks her about Shannon.

"Don't know a Shannon," the woman says. She walks away, into a hotel parking lot.

He hasn't noticed the sheriff's car that's now parked right behind him. A male and a female officer walk to his car, one at each door.

"What are you doing here?" the male officer says.

"I'm looking for somebody." He adds, "Somebody I used to know. Somebody in trouble."

The officers look at each other. The female officer says, "May I see ID? Registration, too."

He complies.

The female officer walks back to the police vehicle.

The male officer says, "If you're clean, you can go." He stands just inches from Gil's car, hand over a gun on his hip.

The female officer returns his driver's license and registration to him. "Go on home," she says. "It's late."

Where is "home"? he thinks. His familial home is no longer a home. His father no longer lives there. His mother can barely maintain the house, even with Gil's meager help. The house he owned with Ceci never did feel like a home. Where is my home? he thinks. To the officer he says, "I really was looking for somebody."

"You don't want to know them if they're down here at this time of night," the male officer says. "Drive careful." He and his partner get back in their police car. They hang a U turn and roar off into the night.

Gil is in a haze. He thinks he's driving north toward familiar surroundings but thinks, too, that possibly he's heading south. The sportscaster on the radio talks of the NBA finals, and Gil drives with his windows down, the night air muggy and warm. There are all sorts of other cars on the road. Many of the cars have surfboards on rooftop racks, and some of the cars pull trailers with those pop-up tents on the back, and most of the motorists appear to be heading off on vacation.

He remembers when he was a boy and his parents took him down to Baja California to camp on the beach. In those days he ate, drank, and slept surfing. It was his life. And his parents indulged him. He met a bunch of other teens who were camping with their parents as well. He remembers surfing the slick dusky waves in the afternoon glass-off, and then later the kids would drink rum and Coke. A few times Gil's parents went into Ensenada with other parents for a night on the town. He slept on the beach in his sleeping bag on those nights.

It was on one such night, after drinking rum and Coke, that he walked down the beach with a girl named Linda. She was Gil's age, fifteen, and she was leaving in the morning, but he didn't know that detail. It was a lovely August night, the sky pregnant with salt air, and the waves splashed a phosphorescent concoction into the black night sky. When they began messing around, he was surprised that Linda let him do anything he wished: put his hand under her bra; leave his hand between her legs for longer and longer; stick his hand underneath her panties; and finally remove all of her clothes. He touched her anywhere, everywhere.

It was over quickly, for he was only fifteen years old and had much to learn about the female body, and about his own sexuality. Somehow Linda and Gil became shy in each other's presence after the very intimate act of coupling on the still warm sand. They walked back along the deserted beach to the campground. When they parted, Linda kissed him and held him tightly. "I'm leaving tomorrow," she said. And she did. He waved to her as she disappeared in her parents' station wagon, wedged in the back seat among her brothers and sisters. They lived in some part of Los Angeles, but he and Linda didn't exchange addresses. They both knew in their adolescent hearts that their night on the beach was inevitable, if not with each other, then with someone else.

He drives on, stuck in his lane. Nothing unusual in that. He's been driving the freeways since he got his driver's license. Freeways are an indelible part of his personal history. He can remember the first time driving on the newly opened 608, the brand spanking-new Freeway North, as it's called, the one that could take them—Gil and his parents; he was an only child—to East Los Angeles from Seal Beach to visit his grandparents. Formerly they took Studebaker Road north and then surface streets until they connected with the Santa Ana Freeway, the 5, which would take them to the outskirts of his grandmother's neighborhood, just off Whittier Boulevard. He also remembers the newly opened 405, the San Diego Freeway, which he caught on the edge of the field behind his house. He still smiles when he thinks about getting to his first job out of high school, which was faring sailboat keels, and how he was able to sleep until seven in the morning, get up, dress, hop on the new freeway, and drive the ten miles south to his exit and be on time for work at seven-thirty! Freeways are wonderful, in Gilbert's opinion.

And this: He spends a good part of his life on them. That's the way it is for Gilbert Padilla and the billion other geographically connected souls who inhabit southern California.

Gilberto Padilla drives the freeway.

The sun is rising over the hills to his left, and in this manner he knows that, yes, he is indeed driving south. Away from his family. Away from relationships both past and future. Toward the unknown.

Gil is stuck in some sort of cosmic dance, some sort of primal car consciousness, heading the direction he doesn't wish to go. Other vehicles hold families. Boys and girls. Men and women. Newborns and toddlers. Humans. Traveling in their machines.

The real stuff happens when they shed their machines. When they press their bodies together and poof! a new human appears. Just like that!

The morning air is hot and humid, with a stiff south wind blowing, and it feels like summer. With all the windows rolled down, the breeze buffets his hair as he speeds south in the arterial-like cluster of vehicles. His vision is blurred and his cheeks are wet for some reason, and still he has a slight feeling of expectation deep in his gut, flying along the roadway, waiting for his car to run out of gas so that in this fashion his forward momentum might cease.

Hard Shoes, Bagged Bagels

I met Harold first. He has a business card with a martini glass as logo, which I sort of like. So when I see him on a small side street in Puerto Prieto in front of a duplex where I did some work for him, I decide to say hello. But he's embroiled in a fierce argument with Danielle, to whom I've not been formally introduced, though I've seen her around town and at the beach and know she's living in Harold's duplex rent free until she finds a job. She's petite, looks eighteen, and seems to have a temper that won't quit.

"You're the kind of Jew who gives Jews a bad name!" she screams at Harold.

"It's for your own good," Harold says. He searches around for an opening, a segue into something else, when he spots me.

I'm making a getaway.

"Guillermo!" Harold says, far too much enthusiasm in his voice. He approaches with outstretched hand; we shake. Danielle glares at Harold, arms akimbo.

"Let me introduce you to my daughter," he says, then adds, "Did you know they made army pants for midgets?"

"Fuck off, Harold," Danielle says, stomping up the small stairway into her house.

"That was Danielle," Harold says while gathering his lawnmowing tools.

I look up at the sky, watching the marine layer begin its daily retreat back over the ocean. I'm waiting for the sun to emerge before body surfing. I'm also out of work but don't care. "I've come at an awkward time."

"She's just like her mother. And I couldn't live with her."

She's your daughter, I think, and you don't have to live with her. Feeling uncomfortable for having intruded upon some sort of familial battle, I begin to make my exit.

"Come in the garage," Harold says. "I want to show you something."

I follow him up the slight incline into the garage, where a car is covered with one of those blue plastic tarps. In a flamboyant gesture Harold uncovers a sixty-six Jaguar XKE. It's white, polished to a sheen, with chrome wire wheels and that wonderful elongated round body.

"Yeah," I say.

Danielle reappears in the garage doorway and says, "I don't want you coming around anymore, Harold. I'll mow the lawn from now on. And I want to park *my* car in the garage."

"Danielle," Harold says, "why do we fight?"

"'Cause you're an asshole."

She now wears a huge T-shirt over a bathing suit, I guess, since all I can see is her tan and well-muscled legs. She also carries a beach bag and chair, obviously on her way to the water.

We're on a small bluff overlooking Puerto Prieto, and some of us, Harold and I, have been here since long before the real estate boom, so even though we don't have much cash, we live in the lap of affluence: ocean breezes, expensive cars, large old beach houses.

The old houses are my forte. I've made a name for myself remodeling and have just come off a two-year word-of-mouth stint. Thus my nonchalance over currently not working.

Later that afternoon Danielle's and my paths cross again. This time we speak as we sit watching the surf break. She tells me that Harold completely unglues her; I tell her not to worry about it, that certain people have the same effect on me. And before sunset we walk all the way to Ladder Rock, where I ask her out to dinner. She accepts, and that night we become lovers.

Danielle's mother's condo overlooks the bay. From the open balcony window you can feel just the slightest bit of autumn waft in on the breeze, a nuance only a Californian would appreciate. We have come to her mother's for dinner so I can meet her. Danielle's brothers also. Since Harold has given me the okay (he didn't object when it became common knowledge that Danielle and I were dating, though I'm still apprehensive about the age difference), I'm accepted by the brothers. Her mother seems fine with my presence too, and dinner has gone well. Gary and Sheldon, the brothers, are out on the balcony, Gary having a cigarette. Danielle and her mother are in the kitchen getting dessert. I'm plopped on the couch watching a television reporter blather on about the PLO.

Danielle's mother, Jean, comes out of the kitchen carrying a tray with coffee on it. She stops before me, saying, "Please, Guillermo, take some."

It's odd, I think, that under different circumstances I might be dating Jean, though she would be the older one. She's taller than Danielle yet still quite small, and her face is almost perfectly sculpted. She's had numerous plastic surgeries to achieve this effect, gifts from a former boyfriend. Dating does seem to have its perks: tuneups if you date a mechanic; gourmet meals if you date a chef; building if you date a carpenter. I'm building a spa gratis for Danielle at Harold's condo.

"Coffee's good," I say to Jean. Espresso from her own machine.

"Are you married?" she asks me.

I gulp down my coffee so I won't choke. Without laughing, I set the cup and saucer on the table. "No."

"Divorced?"

"No."

"Children?"

"No." What is this, Irish questioning? I think.

"Okay, I'll get to the point. Are you of marriageable quality?"

"C'mon, Mom," Gary says from the balcony in a nasal Detroit twang, which is where they are from.

Entering the room from the balcony, Sheldon says, "Look, they're showing film clips from *Exodus*."

"Jesus," Danielle says, returning to the living room carrying a tray with pastries and fruit. "It was such a bore. And you and Harold woke us up to watch it."

"Did we?" Jean says.

"Look," Gary says. "Sal Mineo."

For some reason they all laugh.

"I couldn't stay awake," Danielle says. She sits next to me on the couch.

Jean hands out coffee and pastries to her children. She smiles at me. I'm frightened.

Later, after we've left Jean's and are walking along the bluff overlooking the beach, I say to Danielle, "What's with your mother?"

"She's nuts."

"I know that, but I was referring to all her questions."

"What did she ask you?"

"If I was married, if I had kids, if I was divorced."

"Oh, shit."

"Does she do that to everyone?"

"She doesn't meet everyone."

"I guess I'm lucky."

Danielle takes hold of my hand, placing both her small, warm hands around mine. "She thinks I'm pregnant."

"Who?"

"Jean."

"Who's pregnant?"

"She thinks I am."

We stop and sit on a bench at the point. Across the bay gigantic waves are breaking over the far jetty. The spray from the surf gives a surrealistic tinge to the moonlight. Smaller waves make their way into the channel, where they break in perfect small lines.

"Why does she think that?"

"She says a mother can tell."

"Mother's intuition."

"Well, there's more. I've had morning sickness. And look." She stands up from the bench, placing herself in silhouette. She runs her hands over her stomach. "Things are getting larger."

Danielle, though tiny, is voluptuous. But I don't have a gauge from which to judge change, since we've dated such a short time.

"Don't worry, it's not yours or anything."

"Oh, that makes me feel great."

"I don't mean it like that."

"How do you mean it?"

She sits back on the bench, scooting close to me. "I don't know," she whispers in my ear.

I don't often get visitors, so when a car stops outside my house, I get up to see who's there. Harold stands at the door to my enclosed front porch, his XKE gleaming in the early afternoon sun.

"Come in," I tell him.

He throws down his cigarette, squishing it into the grass, and enters my house. Harold's twenty years older than I, ten years older than Jean. He has a gray tinge to his skin.

"How are things, Guillermo?"

"Fine," I say. Then add, "Work's slow."

"That's what I came to see you about."

"Work?" I always made good money with Harold.

"You know you set me up with Robby, right?"

"Yeah."

"How close are you?"

"Not very."

"I'm going to make him sweat."

"Why?"

"He came in at twenty-five hundred to re-cover the house on Opal Street. You know that property?"

"Yeah." I built a patio cover there a while back. "So what's the problem?"

"He says he made an error taping the roof and he's short material. He wants more money."

"Is he by the hour?"

"No. He bid it."

"Well, you can't have it both ways," I say, though I know Robby is going through bad times right now. His marriage is over. And he has a child. "How much more does he want?"

"Five hundred."

"You're not obligated to pay if you guys had a contract."

"There's nothing in writing."

"You know what I mean."

"Yeah. Let's take a ride. You got time?"

I was reading a mystery. I already swam my two miles in the bay. So we get in his car and head up the coast. Things are much quieter now that school is back in session, not as much traffic, or so it seems to me.

Harold stops in front of his rental property. I look at the roof. It's a three and twelve pitch, not much slope to it.

"How many square did he figure in his bid?"

"Fifteen."

"He's light." I can tell without actually taping the roof. Something you pick up.

Harold starts the car again, and the engine purrs that solid Jaguar hum as we head inland, finally stopping at a bagel shop. I order a garlic bagel with lox cream cheese. Harold pays. We sit in a shade-covered patio.

"The thing with Robby," Harold says, "is he needs to learn a lesson."

"Too bad," I say.

"He's not trying to screw me?"

"He's not that bright."

Harold nods. "I'm going to give him more money for material so he can finish the job. But when he's done, he's going to wait a long time before he gets the last draw."

That's the way it goes: When you most need something, you won't get it. "It's going to be hard on him. He's low on money."

"When you're doing business, you put on your business hat. When you're with friends, you put on your friendship hat. It's that simple."

Harold finishes his bagel, takes a sip of coffee, and lights a cigarette. His voice is gravelly and he has that slight smoker's cough, and he's overweight.

"It's not my concern, really," I say. But I know I can kiss off the two hundred fifty finder's fee Robby owes me.

"No, but you'll hear about it and I wanted you to know my version. It's a small town."

"Fair enough."

He's switched hats, I suppose, for out of nowhere he says, "Don't ever get bagels at the market. Get them fresh, where they make them."

We finish our coffees and then drive down the coast in the early afternoon sun, all the way to Lagunitas Restaurant, where we start drinking margaritas. Below us on the empty beach seagulls lift off the sand, floating over trash. Pelicans skim the backsides of waves, looking for surf fish. A few tourists walk along the promenade.

After my fourth margarita I say, "What were you guys fighting about that day?"

"Danielle and me?"

"Yeah."

"The guy she's been living with. I told her he wasn't welcome at the apartment. He's a creep. And a smuggler."

"Smuggler, eh?"

"Not what you're thinking. Birds. Exotic birds from South America. I told her if he came around, she was out."

"And she wouldn't agree?"

"She lived with the nitwit since she was sixteen. She said it was too hard to be without him."

Harold switches to martinis and I switch to beer. Later we eat fish tacos. When I get home, Danielle is asleep in my bed. She's climbed in through the open window.

"Your closet is so pristine," Danielle says.

We're attending a wedding together, our first outing as a couple for everyone to see.

"I never have a need to dress up."

"But my god, you only have the black suit. And no shoes."

"I have hard shoes." On a shoe rack on my closet floor I have numerous pairs of expensive tennis shoes. And any number of work boots. There's only one pair of dress shoes—black brogues.

"What are you talking about?"

"You know what I mean."

"No, what do you mean?"

"Shoes with hard soles."

"Oh."

Danielle looks lovely. She's wearing a navy blue silk wraparound dress with navy heels. Her hair is up, and she has pearl studs in her ears. She's also wearing makeup. Blue eyeliner and red lipstick and even some rouge on her cheeks.

"The ceremony starts in half an hour," she says, looking me up and down.

I'm still in sweat pants. "It's only five minutes away."

A surf cat we both know has struck pay dirt. He's marrying the granddaughter of a wealthy developer. The surf cat is one year older than Danielle. She knew him in high school. I periodically hire laborers, and I draw from the local surfers-who-don't-want-work-full-time. I hired the groom for a kitchen remodel a while back, thus our individual invitations. The groom has told us all to wear our best clothes and to be on good behavior because he's still trying to impress the developer. The groom won't impress the developer. The marriage will last only eleven months before it's annulled, but he'll get a sound studio out of the deal, which is what he wants in the first place. To be a sound engineer.

All I can do is look at Danielle and wonder what color are her panties. This thought drives me through my shower and propels me while I dress. I watch her sitting on my hassock in the living room, reading a magazine. She crosses her legs and moves her foot to the beat of imaginary music. I notice she's painted her nails. Come to think of it, her toenails are colored as well.

"What are you thinking?" I ask, leaving my bedroom, tying my tie.

"About school."

She's in a Ph.D. program studying comparative literature. On full scholarship. She'll take her master's at the end of this year. She graduated early from high school.

"What about it?"

"If I should drop out or not."

"Don't do that."

"Things are getting complicated."

"Life's complicated."

"But this moment in *my* life is extremely so."

"'Moments' are always complex. Always."

"I've been so incompetent."

"Why?"

"I'm pregnant."

She is. I can see her stomach protruding underneath her silk dress. Not much, but growing nevertheless. And her breasts are fuller too. She has gotten herself in a mess. I don't know if she wishes to keep the baby or not, if she wishes to get back with the father, her former boyfriend, or not. Or where our relationship is heading.

I lean down and kiss her. She stands up. I pull her to me in a strong, supportive hug. She hugs back, then lets go and steps onto the hassock. I untie her wraparound. Blue panties. She unzips my pants.

"I knew the tie would charm you."

"It's pointing to hard shoes," she says.

We miss the entire wedding ceremony and part of the reception. Jean and Gary and Sheldon and Harold are all there, though not together. It's a large wedding, the entire town here, taking place right on the bay at a restaurant.

When the bride and groom leave, they do so by yacht, embarking behind the dance floor set up on the dock. The captain pulls on the air horn. The bride and groom wave. Danielle cries.

Danielle asked me to drive the car. They're all in agreement about this. Harold loved his car. Three nights ago he had a heart attack in his sleep and didn't awaken. The woman he was living with called the paramedics. Danielle's family was called. I spoke with her and then went to the hospital in the wee hours of the morning.

Now I'm driving down the Coast Highway, heading south in Harold's XKE, wearing my suit once again. Even though it's damp in the early November night, the top is down to keep my head clear. For some reason Danielle's family wants Harold's car at this function tonight, this thing they call sitting shivah. I translate it into terms I might understand because I'm hurting too. The best analogy I come up with is the night of the rosary. Except the way they do it, it goes on for seven days.

On my right the ocean is calm, slick, and glassy. Houses fill the hills on my left. People eating dinner, watching television, hanging with their kids, all the things we do as a culture, all the things that define us as a people.

I'm driving to this out-of-the-way house because a friend of Jean's has offered it for tonight to accommodate all those who will be attending. When I finally arrive, the street is full of cars. But there's a spot in the driveway for Harold's. The first thing I notice upon entering the house are numerous plastic bags with bagels in them, probably from Von's, arranged on a table. It takes some time before Danielle and I finally connect, and when we do she falls into my embrace.

"Thanks," she says.

I don't know if she's thanking me for being there or for driving Harold's car or for the hug, but I don't question. I just hug. I hold Jean too, and shake hands with Gary and Sheldon. All of them have red eyes. The house is standing room only, clusters of people everywhere, some of them eating, others drinking, still others consoling each other in quiet tones.

After Danielle has given me a plate of food, something wonderful happens. People all gather in the living room and begin telling stories about Harold. The first man to speak is Harold's best friend, John, an American of Arab ancestry. His weeping interrupts the story, so someone else takes center stage in the large and elegant living room, someone who tells about Harold's adolescence in Brooklyn, before he moved to Detroit. Some of the stories are humorous, some poignant, but every one of them celebrates an aspect of Harold's existence, which makes us feel better.

During the time of storytelling, Danielle's ex-boyfriend arrives. He's really large, though soft when you get down to it. He's been drinking, and Danielle tells me she's going to speak with him in the study. I feel uneasy about this, but don't know what else I can do, given the circumstances, so I remain in the living room. Sheldon catches my eye, gently shaking his head.

After quite some time there's a big crash from some other part of the house. Gary and Sheldon and Harold's best friend, John, arrive in the hallway the same time as I. Danielle is outside the closed study door, weeping. There are more crashes from inside the study. John opens the door, and the ex bellows out how much he loved Harold and why can't he be a part of this? He next takes a chair and throws it against the wall, making a nice hole in it. This is followed by him overturning the desk. Without talking, Gary and Sheldon and John move forward in a pincer-like effect in an attempt to keep him from further destroying the house.

"Calm down," Gary says.

Behind me in the accumulation of people crowding the hall, I hear Jean tell her friend who owns the house to call the police. Danielle is nowhere around. Everybody remains in their positions, like opposing magnets repelling each other into some sort of stasis. In a ridiculously short amount of time, two burly police officers arrive, asking the ex very politely to please go outside, which he does willingly.

People in the house are sort of stunned that this violent and ugly display has occurred at such an inappropriate time. The storytelling has ceased, and once again people are milling in small groups.

Since I can't find Danielle and since curiosity has gotten the better of me, I make my way out to the front of the house. Now is the time the ex decides to fight. He swings at the cop closest to him, but these guys know what they're doing, and the sluggish drunk swing is used to turn the ex around and slam him to the asphalt.

More grievers overflow onto the walkway until it seems everyone is outside getting a glimpse of the show. I'm at the edge of the driveway when I finally see Danielle huddled against Harold's car, shivering. She looks at me for a moment and then back at the ex. ·

His face is pushed against the street, his mouth distorted into a strange and ugly shape. He ceases resisting the cops while they put handcuffs on him.

Danielle will follow the police car to the station, where she will bail him out. They will go to Danielle's house together. In the ensuing weeks they will break up once again, and Danielle will have an abortion. I will fetch her, wobbly legged and groggy, from the procedure. The ex will smarm his way back into Danielle's life, marrying her, getting her to drop out of school, and still the marriage will not work.

"Why are you doing this to me?" he bellows into the night, his sad, pathetic voice echoing off the damp blacktop. Later, while trying to sleep, I will remember that question and that time, resonating like the sound of tires snapping over the rain-slicked streets outside.

Work:
Number
Two
(Tolerance)

The tracts are as large as small cities—the biggest tract you've ever worked on. And they're everywhere in the huge flat area before the mountains. The entire valley is filled with workers and construction equipment, and this is the fastest-growing place in the nation, for God's sake! So decreed *Time* magazine. If there were light, you could work eighteen hours a day, seven days a week, if you wanted. And they still need more bodies.

The framing contractor you work for has a tract that is so big you have to drive to where the catering truck comes for lunch. Fifteen hundred houses in this phase. And you're surrounded by other tracts run by other framing contractors peopled by other tradesmen.

This job is so big there's a rumor that a feud has begun between drywall and roofing. You know the rumor is true because you're working alone, doing soffits and chimney pop-outs and arches, when all of a sudden there are five guys in your work area. You're doing a kitchen soffit. Inside. The guys are drywall men. You can tell by their hands and clothes, which have white dust all over them.

You a roofer? one of them says.

Quick, these drywall guys. The keen eye of the drywall man. Carpenter, you say.

See any roofers? another says.

You shake your head and make a cut. Drown them out with noise. But when the saw stops, there's only silence and wind blowing over the slab and they're still there, watching you.

It's like this, a drywall man says. Some roofers kicked the shit out of our friend. We're going to get them. You sure you're not a roofer?

I'm not on the roof, am I? you say.

He ain't no roof queer, one of them says.

They still look at you. Look at your tools. Not quite believing that you're not a roofer. They want to kick some ass, and they don't much care if it's yours or someone else's.

You see any roofers you tell them we're around, one of them says.

You're on the ladder installing soffit. Gotcha, you say. When you finish the house, you move far away from this area, out of the sequence in terms of where you're supposed to be on the tract, but you don't give a shit; you don't want to be near those maniacs.

You set up all the way at the far end of the tract, abutting the cyclone fence of the next tract. And when you leave that night, it's a desolate and fierce feeling in your gut, something you don't much like, but there it is, part of life.

The next day when there are more people around, you don't feel so vulnerable working alone. Besides, carpenters are competitive, especially pieceworkers. The tract behind you is a union one, and your guys have complete disdain for unions, though they'd love to have the benefits. You know an electrician who gets every other Friday off, paid. Now that's a benefit. But you also know you're paying for this guy to sit on his ass that Friday. Somebody's paying for it.

I could frame circles around your fat ass, a framer might say to another framer. Who taught you how to joist? Your old lady? a joister would say to another joister. Come back when you learn how to use a saw, a siding man might say to another siding man. And so on. So the competitive streak between a non-union job and a union one is intense. The union guys think the non-union guys are scabs who don't know shit. The non-union guys think the union guys are strokers, guys who can't make it pieceworking, thus their hourly cushion.

Not only is the job behind your tract union, but word's out that there's a female framing crew working there. For days everyone has been trying to see them. There have been rumors of a sighting here and there, but no real confirmation. Nobody's seen them working.

Until this one day. They're framing right behind the house you're working on. It's embarrassing when a woman shows up on the job. The yells are reminiscent of teasing girls in elementary school. Except the teasing is more taunt, and the double entendres fly around like gum wrappers in a stiff wind. You've seen realtors run off the job with all the wolf whistling and hooting and hey mamas!

This day you're piecing drop ceilings out of sequence to get away from drywall. You're making good money, gravy, except this day the women framers are right behind the house you're working on. It's as if you're the host for an open house or something. Every asshole framer on the job has to traipse right through your working area to see the women.

There are a few problems, however. Problem number one: The women framers, and there are three of them, are on the slab at virtually the same time as another crew (obviously all male). Problem number two: The women are big and strong, bigger than you, every one of them, and could probably eat you for lunch. Problem number three: The female framers are black. Two young ones and an old one. And they can hump. They detail their house before the guys next to them do. They start nailing perimeter walls bam bam

bam. They're using custom hammers, rigging axes with claws welded on the backs, big heavy ones, and they can set a sinker with one flick of the wrist, the way you're supposed to. And when they nail walls, they cross their legs over, with the opposite foot holding down the stud so it doesn't flop around—taught well, these women. They're efficient, wasting no energy. They don't fuck around. Their perimeter is standing by the time the other crew is finished detailing.

At first the guys who come to the work area are loud, obnoxious, but after word gets out what's going down, most guys are silent. At first it's, Where's the bitches? Can the cunts frame? Stuff like that. Then it's, Shit, they shouldn't allow women on a job. Fuck, what's this world coming to? And on and on.

In the early afternoon, when one of the young women is walking top plate, nailing and putting in backing, and the crew next to them is still on interior walls, the guys stop coming over. You're able to finish the house. Usually you do two a day, but you've been on this house about three hours longer than expected. All the interruptions.

When the female crew rolls up to move on to their next house, only you and the foreman are there to see. It's a cool day, not temperature wise, it's just a cool day. You're dressed in surf work attire— short pants, white crew socks, tennis shoes, no shirt. The women wear Levi's with cuffs rolled over their heavy work boots, long-sleeved denim work shirts, and bandannas over their heads. One of them gives the slightest wave, no smile, as she gets in the truck. You give her the peace sign.

The foreman doesn't mind that you've moved, ignoring tract sequence. Stay away from drywall and roofing, he says. He likes you.

You'll roll up early—fuck it, there's always tomorrow. This afternoon there's the beach, rough and wet and pacific.

Easy
Time

Kick for the *huevos* and cover your face!" yelled Alex, his head slightly moving, tensed and deliberate, like a cat watching a bird.

Tony circled again. He stopped, planted his left leg, and kicked for his uncle's crotch. His uncle shifted minutely, taking the kick on his hip, spun, and kicked Tony hard in the ass. Tony, while turning to face his uncle, saw only the hooded cobra on the back of Alex's hand coming at him.

The cobra hit its mark, this time crisply, and Tony went down. Immediately his uncle was over him, knees bent, fists clenched, like a warrior. The cuffs on his slacks and hard shoes were covered with dust. He wore no shirt, and his upper body rippled with tattooed life: The beautiful Mexicana with long black hair and five black tears heaved in and out on Alex's chest as he stood over Tony. Black snakes on Alex's arms vibrated, writhing and twisting as blood traveled through them.

"You think you're a man? C'mon, get up! You want to fuck up? C'mon," Alex taunted.

Tony climbed to his feet. He slowly circled, stalking his uncle, looking for an opening.

"Close your mouth, stupid! Didn't your old man teach you nothing?"

Darting in at Alex and then backing off, Tony came in fast, throwing his punch. Alex danced with him, forward and back, and when Tony delivered the blow, Alex blocked it with ease and countered. The cobra snapped out quickly, then stopped on Tony's face, just barely hitting so that no real damage was done, but leaving a mark.

He dropped his hands to his sides. His face stung from different hits, and his hair was dusty and his shirt sweaty, caked with dirt. He looked to the sky and saw clouds skittering sideways, pink with sunset.

"Look, Tony, if you're scared, I'll go in with you," said Alex. "I'll call my P.O. and tell him I can't find work, I might screw up. I'll go in with you."

"No. I'll take care of myself."

"I'm going to be honest with you," Alex said. "Whatever happens, don't *run*. If you need help, go to the brothers; they'll protect you. And remember, don't talk to the man. Another thing, don't wear those bun huggers. You got some boxer shorts? I'll bring a pair in the morning."

"It's okay. I've got some. What time you coming?"

"I'll be here at eight." Alex walked up to Tony, embracing him. "Hey, Tony," he said, walking out to his car, fanning himself with his sleeveless shirt, "you'll be all right. You're looking at easy time. It's nothing."

Alex was suddenly gone, and Tony stood there with the boxing gloves still on. As he removed them he thought of his father and he thought of his brother. His father had made Jimmy and Tony "spar," but really they were supposed to fight because they only "sparred" when they were bickering. Jimmy would hold his punches, which infuriated their father. He would take the gloves from Tony, then go at it with Jimmy, leaving him bleeding. Tony would unlace the boxing gloves for his brother, trying to stop the blood that should have been his.

He walked to the front of the house, which was on a small mesa overlooking the ocean. Far off, the sun was a golden yellow coin fading into the sea. The clouds were coral in front and cold gray in back, the color of steel. October, the sky was chilled, the sand below was dark, wet, and the foam of breaking waves was lighting up the beach in small explosions. He sat on the lawn in front of the guest house. The guest house was his, his and his mother's, now that his father had moved out. He thought of the old days when Jimmy was still alive, the autumns when hunters would come and sometimes the big shots would drink too much and kill pelicans and gulls. Nobody cared about sea birds anyway. He had always thought it strange that the guest house faced the ocean and overlooked the tidal marsh, while the hunting lodge, which should have had the better view, faced the road. Tony watched the sky darken and felt the land breeze start to blow, cooling his drying sweat.

In the house he turned on the lights. He climbed the stairs to the loft and bent his head as he entered the low-ceilinged room. It had been the summer before tenth grade when it became necessary for him to bend forward to enter his room. At school the football coach used to get him out of class, bring him hot chocolate, and talk about the team, how they could use him at split end. He liked missing class and talking with the coach; Jimmy had been on the very same team. But in those days he was in Asia, those days he flew a helicopter. The reason behind Tony's refusal was a simple one: He spent his afternoons with Sylvia. Afternoons with the team would be afternoons without Sylvia. Afternoons without Sylvia would drive him crazy. Finally the coach stopped coming to the classroom door. Tony smiled, thinking of high school, ducking his head.

In the added-on bathroom, he showered in the tiny metal stall where there was just room enough to soap himself. Then he dressed and left a note to his mother. As he walked down the dirt road past the hunting lodge, he heard the dry cornstalks crinkling in the wind. They should be turned under by now, he thought. His father used to work the fields in that old John Deere, turning the cornstalks under the soil in thick heavy furrows. Gradually the fields had become smaller as tracts of houses crept up to the ocean, surrounding the hunting lodge.

That was before Jimmy died, before his father moved out with that woman. Then the stables up by the road were sold and so was the hunting lodge and all the surrounding land, but nothing had come of it. About six months ago a helicopter landed right in the strawberry fields. Men wearing suits got out and walked through the neat rows that were then already filled with weeds. When they left, they flew over the marsh again and again, and the rotor cutting the air with that whump whump sound upset Tony, and Sylvia put her blouse on, as if the men above could see through the roof.

Tony crossed the road, heading toward the Colonia, only about a mile inland. It was an old neighborhood completely surrounded by expensive tract homes. There were still roosters and pigs in the Colonia, and on the big holidays they would make *carnitas* in the old copper vats.

He walked on to his grandparents' house. Even though there was a chill in the air, his grandfather had all the windows and the front door open. He was sitting directly in front of the television set with the volume turned way up, watching wrestling on KMEX.

"Hello, Grandfather," Tony said in Spanish.

The old man smiled at him, showing the gap in his front teeth; his incisors looked like fangs without the accompanying front teeth. When Tony went into the kitchen, he saw his grandmother washing dishes with the sleeves of her pink sweater rolled up. He bent down to hug her, surprising and delighting her all at once.

"Are you hungry?" she asked.

"Starving."

It seemed comical to Tony how small his grandmother looked as she walked to the refrigerator and took out some *chorizo*. She shuffled back to the stove, clapping her yellow house slippers, which were too big. She cut off a large chunk of the orange sausage, placing it in a cast-iron skillet, which she then set over a burner on the stove. Soon the sausage was talking through the rising steam, spitting and cracking, filling the air with a spicy aroma.

"Have you seen your father?" she asked.

"No."

"You won't go and see him?"

"I'm not going to that house." That house was the house his father shared with his girlfriend.

"And your mother?"

"She's okay. She's barely speaking to me."

Leaving the stove, his grandmother stood in front of him at the dinette. "She's scared to lose you," she said, stroking his hair.

"I know," Tony said.

"What happened to your face?"

"Alex came by, showed me some moves."

"Alex?" she said with a bit of incredulity, shaking her head. "I saw my son more when he was in."

She warmed handmade tortillas directly on the gas flame, deftly flipping them. When each was hot, she rolled beans and *chorizo* into *burritos* with one end tucked into itself and the other end open like a cone.

After Tony ate he went into the living room and sat on the plastic-covered sofa, trying to watch wrestling. When an acceptable amount of time had passed, he left. His grandmother cried as they hugged good-bye.

"Take it easy," his grandfather said in his deepest voice. He knew what it was all about—a long time ago he, too, had spent time in jail.

Recrossing the highway, Tony walked back home, thinking of things to tell his mother. How after getting out, he would work, help her with the rent. And then after saving some money, he would go to community college. He began walking faster toward the house, and upon his arrival he burst in upon that lonely quiet.

There was a note on the back of his note: His mother didn't want to see him. If he wanted to be like his father's family, fine. But she wasn't going to be a part of it any longer. Going to jail doesn't make you a man. She was sorry but she couldn't bear to see him in the morning, to see him leave. She would be at Virginia's.

Tony crumpled the letter, thinking of the big party Payaso's parents had given their son before he went in. Sylvia had let him undo her pants after the party, when they were alone down in the hollows. And there was the party they had thrown for Alex, right here, when he got out, and he and Sylvia did it for the first time, but she wouldn't do it the way that made you pregnant, she would only do it the upside-down way. He threw the letter on the floor, took the white vase from the windowsill, and broke it over the letter.

He knew that a party wasn't really in order for only thirty days, but he still felt hurt that there wasn't even one person with whom he could spend his last night. Sylvia had changed, the same way his mother had changed. He hadn't even talked with Sylvia since the car thing. And that was why he had stolen it in the first place—to visit her at college, to show her how he'd tattooed her name on his biceps.

"I don't think we should see each other," Sylvia had said, standing in front of her dorm. She always had to study now. And she had cut her long black hair that used to be below her waist, cut it off without even asking him! "Stupid!" she had yelled at him for stealing the car, for putting her name on his body. That was the last time he'd seen her. He had driven all night in the car, the white bathtub-shaped Porsche with the small roof that rolled back to let in the sky. Early in the morning he'd had the bad luck of being in a stolen sports car speeding down the empty Coast Highway, the only car on the road, just as it was getting light.

Leaving the house and walking toward the beach, he crossed the marsh on the old pontoon foot bridge and slid down the small dune covered with ice plant, landing in the sand. The tide was high, so there wasn't much beach. The breeze was picking up, blowing off the tops of waves. Tony looked up and could see the dim lights of the guest house filtering through the small windows and he could see the dark outline of the hunting lodge.

How many Fourth of Julys had it been since he had thrown the sparkler that caught the house on fire? Jimmy had climbed on the roof and put out the smoldering shingles before a real fire erupted. His father was drunk, telling navy stories—how with his LCPV he'd landed marines at Tarawa, but many of them drowned before they could hit the sand, what with all their gear, and most of those who made the beach were gunned down. When his father thought the lodge was catching fire, he managed in his drunkenness to douse with the garden hose the coals that were roasting the buried goat.

Now the wind was drying all the moisture in the air, making the stars against the black sky seem even closer. Tony sat in the sand and removed his jacket. The beach stretched for miles to the south where it stopped at the cliffs. To the north the coastline was straight, and then it jutted out in a huge peninsula. Weak lights from the mansions on the peninsula twinkled as if they were stars that money could buy.

The wind felt warm and Tony removed his clothing. Entering the ocean, power-stroking through the small waves, he stopped past the breakers and treaded water on his back, letting the tops of breaking waves rain back on him. Now that the summer swells had gone, the water was cold; the waves weren't big, but at night they seemed bigger, and when the larger waves approached, you could never be ready for them. A wave broke right on top of him, pushing him unexpectedly down. He relaxed, exhaled, and sprang off the bottom, the way Jimmy had taught him to do when they were young.

As he broke the surface, another wave was in the same place, breaking directly above him. He dove again, pushed off the bottom, and swam to the surface. This time he took a huge gulp of air in case the ocean was serious, but she wasn't, so he swam in to shore. The wind made his teeth chatter as he dressed.

He walked back to the house, stopping next to the porch to pick some of the green mint, the *yerba buena,* growing wild there. Inside, he put water on to boil and threw the note and the larger pieces of glass into the trash. After adding mint to the boiling water, he called Virginia's. Her daughter answered the phone—No, they weren't at home. They had been, but went out for coffee.

"Tell my mother I called," Tony said.

In the bathroom he toweled the salt off his body. After running warm water over his hands, he ran his fingers through his hair. Looking in the mirror, he examined the face that no longer seemed to belong to him. The scar on his chin from falling off his bike. The scar above his eyebrow from that fight after the football game when Payaso broke that guy's jaw. His wavy black hair that Sylvia used to stroke.

He returned to the kitchen, where he removed the pan from the flame, letting the boil die down, the tea steep. The wind was strong now, making the old house moan, making the tall palms outside rustle together and drop their big fronds.

Out on the back porch with his hot tea, he rummaged through a tall wooden box. Both his and Jimmy's yearbooks were in the box, and there were trophies, little golden men with big baseball gloves and helmeted men running with footballs. His certificate, framed and in glass, for making the honor roll the semester that Jimmy first went in the army. His mother had been proudest of it.

He kept digging through the box, looking for the velvet bag. It was on the bottom, flattened with years. Taking it out, he felt its softness, its mystery, its strange authority. Opening the bag, he felt Jimmy's medal.

Tony left the house, walking through the cornfields behind the marsh toward the hollows, carrying Jimmy's Silver Star. The hollows were a series of manmade caves, connected to and cut in the mesa, all cement, ammunition depots for the war their father had fought. Now they were empty and forgotten.

The wind was waving and bending the huge eucalyptus trees serving as windbreaks for the fields. The moon was big though not full, the wind unable to displace it. At the first hollow he walked down the cement grade and lit a match. The match went out quickly, so he lit three at once. Gathering some paper trash and lighting it, he thought how dirty and uncared for it seemed down here. He got the paper lit, then went back up and gathered some brush to start a fire.

We kept it cleaner, he thought. He thought of the nights here with Sylvia. The nights with Payaso and Joker and David and their girlfriends. Payaso was doing federal. Joker too. Armed robbery. Who would have thought it? And now David in the service. Tony looked around the small sphere of visibility, seeing all that showed for so many years of his life. Broken bottles and trash leading out of the light.

Suddenly there was a feeling of freedom that surprised him and made him want to do something spectacular. The worst that could have happened was already over: he was going in tomorrow.

From his pocket he took the medal, thinking of Jimmy. Tony had cried in the shower before the funeral and didn't think he would ever stop, until the hot water ran out. The casket had been closed but he knew that Jimmy was lying in there, his nose bleeding, and it wouldn't stop and Tony just wanted to unlace the gloves for Jimmy and stop the bleeding. When the honor guard fired the salute, Tony cried in public, his dark sunglasses unable to hide the tears that covered his face. After that he never tried to excel in school, the empty lost feeling never subsiding. He used to carry on in his head make-believe conversations with Jimmy. Jimmy, you're a good soldier. You got good grades and didn't hang around with the fuck-ups like I do. Fuck school, fuck the army, fuck that war, fuck those Viet Cong. The only thing that had helped the lonely pain that he felt had been afternoons with Sylvia. It hadn't seemed so bad then.

He took a smoldering branch and walked to the cement wall. The heat burned his hand, but he held the branch firm while he wrote his name huge on the wall and dated it with the charcoaled end. He then kicked apart the flames of the fire and walked back up into the wind.

Tony felt something grabbing his big toe. He kicked at it. It grabbed his toe harder and wouldn't let go. He moaned and kicked with his free foot. Now it had both feet. He stretched and opened his eyes and saw his mother at the foot of the bed.

"I'll make you breakfast," his mother said.

He just stared at her in a sleep-drugged way.

"I took the morning off. C'mon, get up."

His mother went back down the stairs. He looked out the small window below the peak of the roof. The windstorm had left a litter of tree trash all about the hunting lodge and guest house. Branches and leaves and even a few junipers were completely down. But the sky was a blue so crisp and clear you couldn't help but notice—it happened only a few times a year. Off in the distance he could hear the rhythmic sound of breaking waves.

Downstairs at breakfast he said, "Who's going to clean up here?"

His mother had made fried potatoes and bacon and eggs and pancakes, Tony's favorite breakfast. "You mean from the windstorm?" she asked, sitting on a stool off to the side of the table, smoking a cigarette. Her hair was black like his and her face was still pretty, although he thought her beauty stunning.

"Yeah, who's going to pick up?"

"Don't worry about it, Tony. I want you to listen to me. I'm moving in with Virginia. I can't be alone here. Please don't worry about the wind." She exhaled cigarette smoke and then reached for her coffee cup. A car pulled onto the gravel outside. "Everything will be here when you get out," she said smiling, but looking hurt.

Alex knocked at the screen door, automatically opening it. His entry into the kitchen brought with it an overpowering smell of Mennen aftershave. He smiled at them. "You ready, Tony?"

"Let him finish his breakfast," his mother said. "You want some coffee?"

"No. You have some orange juice?" he asked, sitting at the table.

Tony tried to eat but his appetite just wasn't there.

After finishing breakfast they drove in separate cars out the dirt road next to the cornfields. Tony was in a Chevy station wagon that belonged to Alex's girlfriend; his mother drove behind in the battered luxury car with three hubcaps missing. She hadn't cried at the kitchen door. She'd simply said, "We'll talk when you come home."

At the two-lane road the cars went in separate directions. His mother waved as she took off for Coast Highway. Alex drove toward the mountains, which were painfully visible. You could see the folds in the foothills, almost imagine the fir trees high up that surrounded the huge basin.

"Ophelia called her brother and they got word to Spider that you're coming in. Look for him when you get out of processing," Alex said. "Hey, c'mon, Tony, you'll be okay."

Tony turned around and saw the blue of the ocean as he looked back, and watched the lodge and house get smaller and smaller.

"Everything's cool, Tony," Alex said. "Did you wear boxers?"

"I didn't wear anything underneath."

"Shit."

"What?"

"Nothing."

"No, what?"

"Just don't let them put you in with the queers."

"I'll be all right."

They drove through the flats that used to be farmland. They drove past shopping malls and homes that they never could buy, no matter how many hours they worked. The streets, the shops, the stores, even the people walking seemed charged with electricity, seemed to have a new life, as if the wind had rejuvenated the land and every living creature.

They drove up to the main entrance to the city within a city. Alex stopped the car right in front of the door, left the ignition running, and got out, walking around to open the door for Tony. The building was all cement gray with no windows, not one, and big, bigger up close than Tony ever could have imagined. On the roof there was a high fence topped with barbed wire.

"Those are the handball courts," Alex said to Tony as they both cocked their heads to the sky. "You'll get good."

Tony got out of the car. Alex embraced him and said to be cool, don't back down from anybody. "If anything goes down, remember, you're from the south. Nothing that heavy will happen, though," Alex said. He walked back around the car, got in, and just drove off, leaving Tony standing there.

He put his hand in his pocket, feeling Jimmy's medal. He squeezed it as one would an amulet, thinking of his brother. How he'd flown back under fire to get his men. He'd simply done it. Stupid kept ringing in his ears, the stupid that Sylvia had called him, the stupid that hurt his mother.

Tony opened the glass doors, trying not to show how scared he was, trying to suppress that lump in his throat, and at the same time realized there was no such thing as easy time.

Lost

Building wooden models of sailboats but thinking about Bonita out there putting up signs at the markets and on the corner stop signs and at the elementary school. She's taped one on the window of my car. It says:

LARGE REWARD FOR WILLIE

BRINDLE MALE PIT BULL TERRIER

VERY FRIENDLY TO PEOPLE

KEEP AWAY FROM OTHER MALE DOGS!

We stayed up late last night making those signs on my workbench where I'm now working. My phone number is listed on the sign and so is Bonita's, but she's here most of the time.

The ribbing for the hull is made out of two-by-four scraps that I get across the street. They're building one of those long skinny houses like they do in Corona del Mar, and it reminds me of a boat in some aspects—the cantilevered front deck looks like a prow cutting through almost tropical air. The first step is to cut the scraps into pieces that will act as bottoms and uprights for the siding "planks," which are, in actuality, thin strips of balsa wood. I put the fir strips in a row and then tie them together with a pin through a balsa wood "plank." It's tedious work, and since I don't know shit about boats, it's hit and miss, but it's something to do. Bonita's roommate, Linda, is making batik sails for it and the deck will be teak. But that's a long way off. And I want this one to be good; maybe then I can get in the Sawdust next summer and quit construction for good.

Trimming long pieces of balsa wood to use as siding for the hull when the phone rings. I live in an old house—probably to be removed as soon as the old lady who owns it dies and her asshole son can make it big on the land sale (and then maybe there will be a big boat right here where I'm sitting). After three years living here, I still get disoriented when I stand too fast. The foundation piers are all rotted, so the house leans to the south, or starboard side, and it feels almost like walking in the fun house when you were a kid.

I walk into the kitchen to get the phone. "Hello?"

"What's happening, Juan?"

"Nothing much."

"Wanna come to my party tonight?"

"Who is this?"

"Billy!"

"Oh. Hi, Bill."

"So do you want to come?"

"I don't know. Maybe I'll be by late."

"Well, stop by. It's gonna be big. We got a band."

"Great. Maybe I'll see you later."

Fuck the Fourth of July. There's just a bunch of drunk assholes throwing firecrackers everywhere. Like last year. Ann, my girlfriend last year, got a firecracker to land right on her foot. It didn't bleed or anything; it just turned all black, I suppose, from the powder exploding. The guy who threw it was really drunk, so what are you going to do?

My workbench occupies the entire back wall of the living room and I set it up level, but unfortunately the very far end is unusable because it drops too far below what is a comfortable working height because the floor drops the most at that point. So that's where I have my stereo and store my woodworking tools.

They were my brother's before he dove into the water right at Punta Banda with a big swell running just to see if he could beat the tidal surge that rushes into the rocks and shoots spray at least twenty feet in the air. La Bufadora. The blowhole. The Federales walked the beaches but finally some American scuba diver recovered the body. I went down with my father and never once looked at it, and my father had to pay over a thousand dollars in bribes to get my brother back onto this side, not to mention the cost of the dry ice.

On the way back into the living room I put on *Motown's Greatest Hits* and blast it. The first song is my favorite—"Heat Wave" by Martha and the Vandellas. My brother once took me to Melodyland Theatre, where we saw the Supremes and Martha on this big stage that went in a circle.

I just get back to the chair when there's a tap at the window.

Jim, my neighbor in back, sticks his head inside my living room through the open window and says, "I've got your money, Juan. C'mon back and I'll pay you."

Why doesn't he just give it to me now? I'm always ready to get money, so I walk back to his house. My grass is dead and bristly from the heat of summer. The sun is starting to break up the overcast, the sky looking like a great gray tarpaulin being rolled back. It's going to get hot again.

I open Jim's rusted screen door and step into his living room. His house always smells like someone's dirty hair, so I suppose that's why I don't come back all that often. Jim, who is tall and in perfect shape from surfing all the time and from pouring concrete for a living, stands and offers me a mirror with four tiny white lines stretched out on it. A straw with a jagged edge on one end almost rolls off the small platter. I sniff one of the lines while Jim holds the mirror for me. He then hands it to his friend who's sitting in the beat-up overstuffed pink couch underneath the open window, where red bougainvillea climbs right in the living room.

"Another Fourth down the tube," Jim's friend says.

"There's nothing to celebrate," a new guy says, walking out from the bathroom. "No waves, man."

"I wanted to thank you for loaning me the money," Jim says to me. "You want a beer?"

"It's still a little early."

"I'll get your money," Jim says, leaving for the bedroom. The guy who was in the bathroom sits in Jim's chair and takes the mirror and snorts a line. Then he starts playing with his nose, wiggling it and making snorting horse noises. "Good stuff," he finally says.

"Thanks again, Juan," Jim says, returning from the bedroom. He hands me the hundred.

"My pleasure."

I smile at the surf cats but they can't see me.

Back at the workbench I really don't feel like working anymore because the coke makes me feel like doing something, anything but concentrating, when the front door opens and Bonita walks in with her roommate, Linda, and Linda's boyfriend, Joe.

"Hi," Linda says. "We've been all over the neighborhood but nobody's seen Willie."

Bonita goes and sits on the couch. She has on a big T-shirt over her bare legs. She flops her long hair on her back in a nervous twitch.

"Maybe we should drive around," I say.

Bonita just looks at me.

I let Willie out about four in the morning three days ago when I couldn't sleep. Sometimes I have trouble keeping my eyes closed, so I get up. Willie wanted out, and I let him go. What's the big deal? I'll tell you. He hasn't returned.

"Juan, you remember Joe, don't you?" Linda asks.

"Yeah. How you doing?"

"Hi," Joe says. He pulls out a plastic bag from inside the waist of his cut-off Levi's. His hair is short with a long tail in back. He's slight, looking as if he's never worked. He walks to the couch, sits there next to Bonita, and takes from the glass coffee table a *Fine Woodworking* magazine, which he uses for a plate and starts rolling joints.

I put my tools neatly in the corner of the workbench, folding the chisel set into the chamois pouch that my brother made for them. I go into the kitchen and get some beers. It's a holiday.

Linda is sitting on the floor beside Joe, and she's taken off her tie-dyed beach wraparound. She's in her thirties, in very good shape, and she's vegetarian. It's funny how she and Bonita are roommates because Bonita is only eighteen. Linda and I used to have mutual friends who were married. But they separated and Linda and I stayed friends, and it was Linda who introduced me to Bonita.

"Can I use the phone, Juan?" Linda asks.

"Sure."

Bonita just sits there, her eyes all watery, staring at the wall. She's short, five two, and is really tanned. She's a waitress at Marie Calendar's, so she gets to go to the beach every day, but right now her bottom lip is sticking out. Joe blows out a smoke ring and passes the joint to Bonita.

"Don't you have any other music?" she asks, taking in a big puff. She pauses for a moment and then says, "How about some Wham?"

Smokey Robinson is now singing about shopping around. "What's Wham?"

"I bought that album for you," she says, standing up and walking over to the rocking chair to pass me the joint.

When she gets right in front of me, I smile and shake my head. She turns to walk it back to Joe but I grab her from behind and pull her on top of me and kiss her neck and squeeze her. Linda comes out of the kitchen and Bonita hands her the joint as she passes us.

"I called my psychic," Linda says, inhaling smoke from the joint, standing in front of Joe.

"What'd she say?" Bonita asks, squirming off my lap.

"She said someone will bring Willie home tonight."

"Couldn't you get an address?"

Bonita shoots me a mean look. That dog is a father-mother-brother-sister all rolled into one for her. He's her best friend and guard dog. He's more dependable than any of her family, and he's certainly been around longer than me, and if he returns he'll be around longer than me.

He's a big tough beast and looks a lot like the dog Petey from *The Little Rascals*. Most of his teeth are missing or broken from fighting and from chewing on rocks. He has the grip that pits have; he won't let go in a fight. I've seen Bonita stick her finger up his ass to get him to let go of another dog before he kills it. In a fight Willie is like a sixty-pound death mouth.

Sometimes after we walked through the little park down on Carnation that overlooks the bay, it would look as if there had been a windstorm because there would be leaves and branches all over the ground from where Willie had hung from limbs, twisting and jerking and pulling and hanging there until the branch fell and he tore it to shreds.

"Wedding Bell Blues" comes on and Linda starts lip-syncing it to Joe. Joe is a lot younger than Linda. Bonita walks to the work-bench, to where the turntable is, and starts looking underneath it through the records.

"He's just after pussy," Joe says, exhaling smoke. "I had a dog that was gone for ten days. One morning I opened the front door and he was laying there like nothing happened." He wets his fingertips and then smashes the fire out of the joint.

"He'll be back tonight," Linda says.

Bonita rejects the record.

Later, as we're driving around in my convertible Karmann Ghia, Bonita says the carob trees lining the streets smell like cum. Then she smiles at me.

We drive down street after street of small, cozy houses with the draperies open to let you see how their decorating scheme looks better than a magazine. The houses are close together; some of the people are mowing lawns or digging in their flower beds, but nobody's seen Willie. I drive up to the stretch behind town where it's still Irvine Ranch land and undeveloped. I get out of the car, walk to the barbed wire fence that is down—pushed over by joggers— and check out the ditch by the side of the road. Nothing.

In the late afternoon we walk to the beach. Bonita and me. I hold her hand. It feels good to have a girlfriend on the Fourth of July.

Big Corona is steaming with people; beach shrieks climb all the way up the bluff and greet us as we begin the descent down to the sparkling water. All of inland southern California is here having barbecues, putting on suntan oil, eating, screaming, kissing, laughing on the beach. There's a traffic jam at the entrance to the parking lot. On the beach below, there's not even any place to spread our towels. In fact, it looks like one of those photos of the French Riviera where the people must all stand because there's no room to do anything else. I go in the water by the low tide rocks so that Bonita will be able to find me. She feels like walking, and in an instant she is lost in the wiggling crowd.

On the way back to my house, we check the park on Carnation. When I get away from Bonita, I check in the bushes because sometimes dogs go off to die.

In the shower Bonita holds me a long time after we've satisfied each other and she cries. I want to tell her that I took off work yesterday and drove to the pound in Huntington, the big one in Orange, and the one out on Canyon Road in Laguna, but instead tell her we'll go on Monday.

Joe and Linda come back from the beach, use my shower, then we all decide to go get something to eat. But first we drive to Costa Mesa to see if Willie has made the long trek back there instead of returning to my house. He hasn't.

So we go to International House of Pancakes. It seems to be the only place open. We all have breakfast, except for Bonita, who won't eat. The service is terrible. The waitress hides every time we want something. And we're the only ones in the huge blue A-frame, and we can't even get our check. Bonita sticks her fingers in her mouth and whistles loud and shrill for the waitress but we all think, hey, that's Willie's whistle.

Outside, Joe says, "He'll turn up."

"He'll be back tonight," Linda says. "We're going to The Annex and have a beer."

Bonita is no way going to get into a bar, even with a phony ID, so we decide to go to the movies. We drive over to Harbor Boulevard. Rates have gone up to six dollars but I refuse to pay that much for a look down a tunnel. Big screens, big sounds, that's something different.

"Let's try the exits," Bonita says. We walk around in back and try the exit doors to see if we can sneak in. Every one is locked.

"Let's go back to your house and see if Willie's there."

"Some psychic," Bonita says on her little couch, sitting next to me, with her new Thompson Twins playing. We're alone in the semidarkness—only the light from the kerosene lamp silhouettes the room. We start kissing. I open her blouse and look at the white part of her breasts, the part always covered by her bathing suit. There's one vein that travels almost to her nipple. Above her breasts she has thousands of tiny sun freckles and when I touch them, for an instant, my fingerprint stays on.

Work:
Number
Three
(Empathy)

Y ou're in your truck with the tools locked safely in the back, your pocket full of bread, and horny as hell. No girlfriends, no relationships, no attachments. But you're up to no good, are going to get laid, going to stick it in somebody's something, and you don't care whose as long as she's available.

On the way to a bar in Costa Mesa. Where a guy you work with got a blow job in the parking lot. You yourself have never picked up a woman in a bar. Sure, you've left with someone before, but it doesn't count because you already knew her. For some the setup works, for others it doesn't. You're one of the ones for whom the dating/mating system doesn't work, though you're the hopeful optimist, thinking tonight's the night.

On the way home from the bar—it's two a.m., closing time, and of course you got nothing, though you did get a phone number because you knew she wouldn't leave with you and you had the good sense not to ask her and your reward was the number, if it's real—you've got to be cool on the road. Everyone knows how Puerto Prieto police are. Be cool.

Just after making the turn onto Pacific Coast Highway from Dover, you notice a hitchhiker. A female! Yeah. You pull over, remembering the time a few years ago when you were living with Serena. Driving home one time, you picked up a woman who was hitchhiking. She'd needed money badly; in fact, she'd offered to blow you for ten dollars.

You've got evil designs, in your semidrunken state. Surprise, surprise, she gets in the truck.

I'm running away, are the first words out of her mouth.

That must mean she's young. Things are looking better and better in your semidrunken state.

I need a place to crash, she says, looking at you expectantly.

You look her over. She's maybe fourteen. You're twenty-six. Sure, you can crash at my place, you say. It's really small, though.

That's okay, she says, I just want to get off the street. She looks at you with relief. She's ordinary looking, sort of nondescript young teen. Short brown hair. Thin. Dirty clothes. Jacket too heavy.

Your criminal sensibility kicks in in your semidrunken consciousness, so you begin driving in circles so she won't know how to find your house again. You're not sure what the logic in this is. But it's after 2 a.m. and seems a good idea. You kill at least twenty minutes driving in circles, until you feel it's safe to take her to your house.

Wow, she says, it sure is small. She looks at the bed that takes up the entire room of the studio apartment.

Take a shower, you tell her.

She obeys, this kid.

You get in your bed in your semi-drunken state. Ceiling spinning. For some reason you remember the time you were hitchhiking when you were a teen.

A February night on U.S. 395, the temperature well below freezing in the desert. You're supposed to get back to work at Mammoth Lakes, the ski lodge. But whenever a car comes, which isn't often, you'll hitchhike in *either* direction—you just want to get out of the biting cold. There hasn't been a car in over an hour. It's getting later and colder and you don't know if you'll make it through the night.

You shouldn't have taken the ride with the farmer. But you were sick of sitting on the outskirts of Mojave. So get moving, you thought. Not a good thought, in retrospect. The desert stretches out in all directions in a rolling white seascape, the moon tells you so.

Some headlights are far down the road, getting bigger and bigger, heading toward you. Petitionary prayer is in order, and you do so. As the vehicle gets closer you see it's a bus—the Greyhound. Fuck hitchhiking, you'll pay! As the bus gets closer you wave your arms above your head. This is not asking for an act of kindness, this is a demand on human empathy to save your life.

Yet you're still surprised when the bus actually stops. Right in the road, not even bothering to pull over.

Get in out of the cold, son, the bus driver says. There aren't any seats, but you can sit on the steps.

Looking toward the back of the bus, you can see that every space is occupied. This is what the guys who work at the lodge call the "fun bus." And you can see why. It's like a big moving party. You can smell alcohol and guys are going in between seats and some people are making out in the back. The Thursday night Greyhound that brings skiers from Los Angeles.

Just when you're ready to park on the steps next to the driver, a voice says, You can sit with us, c'mon.

You follow the voice to your further savior, finding it attached to a high school girl who smiles at you. She stands up. I'll sit on your lap, she says. Take your jacket off.

You've got on an extra-long down parka, one for skiing powder, your down pants, thermal boots, and ski gloves. Your wool cap hides most of your hair but when you take it off, releasing your ponytail, she smiles even more. You're nineteen; she's fifteen or sixteen.

The bus slowly and steadily rumbles forward and the laughter and partying around you seems to come from some inner recess of your mind, as if in a dream. While shivering big time, your savior snuggles and holds you. You sleep with the smell of fresh-washed hair on your face. Your arms are comfortable around her, holding her warmth as you feel her breasts rising and falling with the rhythm of the rocking bus.

Sometime in the night the bus driver yells out, Lone Pine! and the air brakes halt the beast. Your savior kisses you softly on the lips and says, Bye, and she's gone.

This huge feeling of love washes over you. Most of the partyers are now silent, passed out or asleep. You watch your savior walk off the main street in the black and white night, and you realize you don't even know her name. The bus lurches forward.

You doze and wonder about your family and about your job and just doze. The snow on the ground is thicker and blocking the road, and the bus lurches and grabs like a sailboat under sail in heavy seas.

Around two in the morning the bus stops. The driver yells, Bishop! This is as far as we go—road's closed. There's a hotel two blocks up.

Everybody disembarks in slow motion. Snow flurries obscure the iced-off street and this must be above the Arctic Circle.

You know a family on the outskirts of town; you'll try to stay the rest of the night at their house. Before you get too far from the bus you hear, Wait, where you stayin'?

Two women walk up. They're older, maybe twenty-five, and you say you've got a friend in town.

Do you know Ron Kingsly? one says. I've got to get to him.

I know who he is, you say, but I don't actually know him. You work in the unglamorous rental shop, Ron Kingsly works on ski patrol. Some big muck-a-muck.

Can we come with you? the other says. We're low on money.

Okay, you say.

Their names are Penny and Sandi.

You walk to the edge of town to the Wrightman's house, where you've stayed before. One of your friends is in love with the youngest daughter, but he's too old for her and she'll break his heart.

You now knock on the door of the house but nobody answers. You know the guest house is always unlocked and the grandmother lives there. You go to the guest house and knock, but again no answer. So you just walk in the front door.

There are two sleeping bags in the closet, so you give them to Penny and Sandi. Sandi says, You can sleep with me. She's the one going to be with Ron Kingsly. She has red hair.

Why not? It's been such a weird night anyway.

You both get in the bag and immediately start kissing. She lets you feel her soft big tits and her crotch is nice and wet. Things are getting heavy; just before you're ready to climb on, she says, Please, don't.

You're not that experienced, and in fact you've only had real sex with the one girl you loved, your high school girlfriend. And it's been quite some time since you broke up, one of the reasons you're working at Mammoth. Your hard-on is getting painful and all you want is to be inside the soft-warmth called Sandi.

Please, she says again, I'm going to live with Ron.

You kiss and hold her and she kisses your cheek and puts her arm around you and like that you're asleep, even though your desire rages all night.

In the early morning the grandmother is there in the living room, her living room, staring at everyone on the floor. You all scram, out into the early morning Bishop air, feeling great—you've survived the night and Sandi's scent permeates you and it's a glorious snow morning.

In town behind the bakery there's a rack of hot bread in a halo of steam, so you swipe a loaf and split it with Sandi and Penny and then easily hitchhike up the mountain because you're with two women and anyone will pick you up on a wonderful day before the best skiing of their lives.

Your existence is solitary, if not bleak. You share a small trailer out at Old Mammoth with a friend nicknamed Owl, who's like a movie star—a different woman each night. He's never around.

You see Sandi and Penny from time to time but they run with an older, cooler crowd but there's a bond between you, the shared intimacy of a snowbound night followed by the best bread in the whole world. You've talked with Sandi at a couple of parties, and she's come by the rental shop to say hello, the uncool, stuffy ski rental room.

So you're really taken aback when you're awakened one night by a knock at the door and find Sandi there. Her eyes are all red and she's not even got on a parka, just a too small Levi's jacket and no gloves and no hat, and her eyes are all red and her mascara has run.

My mother died, is what she says. She died today and I'm leaving tomorrow. I didn't want to be with Ron, she says. I wanted to be with you.

You get her in the small trailer and proceed to warm her. Rubbing her hands. Rubbing her limbs. Hot tea. A shot of Scotch. Put her in your warm bed and all night she tells you stories of her mother in between crying and shivering.

At dawn you strap on snowshoes and take her to your spot. It's through the meadow and behind the first ridge that ascends to the top of Mammoth Mountain.

Your spot is the quietest place on earth. It's all snow covered and the fir trees are old growth and reach to the sky and the sky it-self is so pristine it makes your eyes tear. If there is a god . . .

The quiet is so complete, so overwhelming, it's like standing at the ocean or at the base of a waterfall, the quiet is so noisy. After a time Sandi says, I knew you'd help.

Sleep must come, at least a few hours, for you to hump joist to-morrow. You don't know whether or not you're awake or dreaming but there's a person backlit by the light of your bathroom and she's wearing your bathrobe but she's somehow too small. You wonder what happened to Sandi and wonder where in the hell is this girl's mother? this teen who's had to run away. The good news is that you're no longer semidrunk.

A Place in France

Leo stopped in Corona del Mar on the way back from work because he knew Diana, his wife, wouldn't be home. They were fighting. She was going to visit her folks for a few days, for the weekend.

The sun was setting as he pulled in front of Bobby's rundown bright pink house. Mirella, the old Italian lady who owned the house and who lived next door, was out in front sniffing carnations. She was bent over, so that her dress was up in back, and Leo saw her huge white haunches above the tops of her knee-length hose. As he stepped from the car, Mirella stood upright.

"Lovely, lovely," she exclaimed.

Standing a few feet from her, he saw that her false teeth were out. She held a clear plastic glass of red wine. The palms lining the street were surrounded by a brilliant blue sky that was a flaming red to the west. Palm frond fingers wiggled in the small breeze of sundown.

Mirella placed her hands on her belly and leaned

back. "Lovely." She sipped from her glass. Then she said, "Bobby's home," motioning to the front door with her free hand.

"Thank you," Leo said. He saw wine remnants just above the corners of her mouth, and this made him think of how children sometimes get milk mustaches or ones of Kool-Aid. When he thought of children, he naturally thought of Diana.

"Go on," Mirella said. She smiled at him so that the corners of her mouth turned up with that silly red coloring.

He passed over the thick dead St. Augustine grass and stepped onto the porch.

Bobby opened the door. "Goddamn right, daddy," he said. He wore no shirt, which showed off his well-defined muscular chest; he was a carpenter, a layout man. He snapped lines all day, delineating where the walls would go on the slab. His hands were permanently red stained from the chalk. Even though the evening was cool compared with the heat of the day, Bobby was sweating.

Leo and Bobby had been friends since high school, and this fact seemed to be the only thread they still had in common, but it was a strong one.

"I'm in the back room. Grab yourself a cold one." Bobby walked to the spare bedroom.

Leo moved into the kitchen. He opened the curved, ancient refrigerator and took a Heineken. That was the only brand Bobby would drink. Leo wasn't so much interested in the *kind* of beer as he was in its temperature. He insisted on cold, very cold, beer. And Bobby's refrigerator kept it slightly above freezing, much to Leo's delight.

In the bedroom on the desk was an old scale of the sort that blind justice used to hold. The kind that would balance everything equally. Two small plastic bags of white powder lay next to the scale.

"Yes, sir!" Bobby snapped from his desk. He moved his head back and said, "Yeah." Then he motioned to Leo with a silver straw; Bobby pointed to the porno magazine in front of him.

Leo thought it would make him feel better. He wouldn't think of Diana. Besides, it was Friday night. He took a line.

After numerous blasts and four beers and after the Angels lost to the Red Sox, Leo left Bobby's. Walking to the street, he looked in Mirella's window. She was passed out on a couch, looking very alone. A huge television shrieked color.

On the empty road between Corona del Mar and Laguna, Leo accelerated his new Bavarian car to well over one hundred miles an hour. He flew past moonlit coves that should have been on travel brochures. His stomach dropped as he slid down the hill at Crystal Cove.

He remembered swimming there one night when he and Diana had been dating. It had been summer. The phosphorous plankton was in. Leo knew the water was in the mid-seventies, the way it always was, like bathwater, toward the end of summer. He and Diana walked along the ocean late one night during a heat wave.

They stripped and entered the water slowly. But then Leo ran ahead and did a head dip, stuck his head below a breaking wave so that he was completely wet without diving in. Diana waded thigh deep.

"C'mon," he yelled to her.

"It's cold," she said.

"It's just right." Even in the dark, and with not a big moon, Leo saw her beauty. She kept in shape running with him three times a week.

A wave approached them and she dove under. She came up laughing, her shoulder-length hair now thin and inconsequential.

He cupped his hands, throwing water in the air, hitting the surface with the flat of his hand, splashing; the ocean glowed with life, like fireflies fluttering up. Diving under, he opened his eyes in the surging silence. With the aid of the glowing water, he was able to find Diana.

Breaking the surface, he said, "Let's swim out."

Diana was a good swimmer, but usually she was afraid to swim in the ocean at night.

"You never answered me," Diana said, getting close to him. Earlier, for some stupid reason, they were discussing past loves. Diana wanted to know how many lovers Leo'd had. He tried to be coy but Diana persisted. He was forced to estimate down a number between twenty and thirty.

At first she was taken aback. And then pissed. But what did she expect? They were older. They both had established themselves in their respective careers. Leo accepted the fact that she, too, had had other lovers.

"Exactly how many?" She wanted a definite number, one that could be assigned.

"I don't remember."

"Tell me what number I am."

What do you tell your wife when she asks what number she is on your totem pole of past loves? A small wave pushed them closer to shore.

"You want a precise number?"

"Damn right."

That was easy. "One."

Leo dove under the surface. With open eyes he saw the zillions of tiny particles that gave the water such a strange glow. Finding Diana's ankles, he pulled himself up her legs, stopping at her thighs, transfixed while watching the infinite spark-like explosions that went off all around her.

He snapped out of his reverie by having a blast. Soon he was in a surreal late-night traffic jam, crawling because of the Laguna Art Festival. Finally wearying of the slow-moving traffic, he pulled into the liquor store at Boat Canyon and bought a six-pack.

Canyon Road was a bottleneck, so Leo sipped a beer that wasn't nearly as cold as he liked it and had another blast.

As he passed Canyon Road, the traffic seemed to clear somewhat, even though it wasn't what you would think it would be at almost eleven at night. Climbing the hill past Fahrenheit 451, the bookstore, he was able to accelerate.

And then all of a sudden he saw the Crazy Lady hitchhiking in front of the Jack-in-the-Box. He remembered how Diana, who had lived across the street from the Crazy Lady, had sung that jingle: "There's a place in France where the women wear no pants." That was what Diana sang when she told Leo about the Crazy Lady.

This old woman, this supposed crazy lady, walked all day. That much was true. Leo had even seen her this morning on his way to work. They say she was from France, that she had lost her husband and son in a fiery auto accident on Laguna Canyon Road, the dangerous link between Laguna Beach and the outside world, so she wandered the streets looking for them. Leo had seen her countless times walking along the side of the road between Corona del Mar and Laguna. He'd seen her as far north as Sunset Beach, as far south as San Clemente.

Once he and Diana were window shopping after they'd bought their condo. The Crazy Lady was walking past a construction site across the street. All the workers began hooting and making dog calls and whistling. The Crazy Lady didn't say anything, but she defiantly took a box of nails that was lying on the ground next to some fresh cement and dumped it right in. And the construction workers shut up. But Leo had never before seen her hitchhiking.

Approaching her, he saw her long white braid trailing after her shaking head as she bawled out cars. She was around sixty, and she wore a long black sweater dress. She was small yet perfectly proportioned, and perfectly animated.

Leo pulled his car over to the side of the street. He leaned over and opened the passenger door for her. She looked at him and, without saying anything, sat in the passenger seat.

"I know where you live," Leo said. "Off Golden Lantern above Dana Point, right?"

The Crazy Lady looked at Leo as if to say, So what? She had a terrific body odor—an odor of moldy almonds, which at first made his throat constrict and the beer come up. He relaxed, the beer went back down, and he felt the cocaine coursing through him once again.

They slowly pulled back into traffic and drove. As they passed Monarch Bay, Leo looked up the hill to his own condo. He thought he saw a light on. Maybe he'd forgotten it this morning. Or maybe Diana had left it on for him?

Leo looked over at the woman. She sat with her jaw set, staring straight ahead, fidgeting with her hands. He didn't try to make conversation. He sipped on his beer from time to time and drove. He drove as if he were going to meet Diana, which he'd done countless times in their courtship. Not certain which apartment belonged to the Crazy Lady, he idled his car forward through the apartment parking lot until she started opening the door.

"Can I use the bathroom?" he asked her. He didn't think that he could make it back to his house.

When she didn't respond, Leo parked and quickly followed her to the apartment, barging in right behind her, just like in the movies, except the Crazy Lady offered no resistance, for maybe she was crazy after all.

All the apartments in the complex were alike, or so Leo assumed, since this apartment he now stood in was exactly like Diana's had been. He made his way to the bathroom. Once inside, he heard footsteps above him—the bathroom was in the stairwell—as she climbed up to the second-floor bedrooms. Leo felt a strange excitement welling up inside him. He was actually inside a complete stranger's house. He felt power. He took a snort of coke.

As he glanced around the bathroom, he had the distinct feeling that he was in a service station restroom minus graffiti. Disgusting kept coming to mind. Long white and gray hairs clung to the obligatory Pullman. The toilet retained a dark ring at the water line that remained naked and crusted when he flushed. The Crazy

Lady's hand-washed undergarments covered the shower curtain rod, old-fashioned garter belts and nylons. Black lace underpants, black bras with frilly edges. He looked at the tag on a bra—34B— and imagined kneading her soft bosom, imagined running his hands over her silky underpants, both front and back. He turned off the light, and the tin-sounding bathroom fan fell silent.

He walked into the kitchen. He could walk into any room he wished and nobody could stop him, he told himself. Without thinking, he opened the refrigerator. Some candy bars, some opened cat food with no covering, and an open bottle of wine were the sole occupants of the huge new refrigerator.

He opened the cupboard above the sink. After rinsing a glass, he poured some wine. It was a cheap white Zinfandel, but it was cold. He sat on one of the leatherette bar stools, wondering just where Diana was this very minute. Outside, a large black cat silently cried through the closed glass door. It kept miming cries, and Leo thought the reason he was unable to hear the cat was a physical one. Yet when he opened the door, the cat still had no voice. It stared at him with a look of disdain before entering the apartment, and when it did, it jumped over the threshold and walked to its bowl in the corner. He took a box of dry cat food from the counter and poured some for the cat. It waited for him to finish, then began devouring the food while its collar clanked against the side of the red plastic bowl.

Leo moved to the bar and sat on a stool. He sipped wine. Taking another snort of coke, he felt power surging through his entire body. American express, he thought, his mind racing.

He thought of his life, which consisted of driving to Los Angeles from Orange County. He was a copy machine salesman, with accounts to service and glad-hand, clients to take to lunch, small acts of bribery to perform daily. The olives to the account in the City of Industry. The Chivas to Tom at Olin's, the Glen Livet to Roger over in purchasing for Sandy's Dress Shops. These were the small bribes.

Some days he left his house at five in the morning, but other days he left well after nine, after traffic had subsided somewhat. It all hinged upon what sort of schedule had been previously arranged. Tomorrow he had no schedule—Diana was gone.

He'd been having an affair and had been caught. The woman's name was Lisa. They were coming out of a liquor store in Laguna, on the way to Lisa's, when a woman blocked their path in the doorway. Leo didn't look at the woman but placed his hands on Lisa's hips and moved her while they giggled. The woman, when Leo finally looked at her, turned out to be a friend of Diana's whom Leo knew and liked. She said, "Hello, Leo," and then walked into the store. He assumed the friend would tell Diana. But when Leo confessed, Diana said she hadn't heard from her friend. Then Diana had an affair with her boss. Leo wanted to think he'd stopped his affair because he loved Diana.

For no reason he lumbered over to the stairs, surveying the house as he stood at the base. The filth, the clutter, the clothes on the table and floor, the disarray was oppressively evident. From the next-door apartment he heard muffled music.

Somewhat shakily, he began to climb the steps. Just to see more. That's what you're supposed to do, he thought, get more. That was the basis of everything. You deserve more. He certainly didn't feel like returning home to an empty condo. So he moved to the top of the stairs while holding on to the black metal railing.

At the top he stopped.

He listened.

Nothing.

Two closed doors faced him. A clerestory window shed artificial light from the outside street lamp onto the top of the stairs. He stood frozen before the first door. Had he been a cat, his fur would have been standing up on his neck like a thick necklace.

He opened the door. The room was dark. It was a small bathroom, and through the open window he heard the sound of pounding surf off in the distance. He turned his attention to the other door. His heart was flying, and a slight perspiration formed on his forehead. He put his hand on the doorknob and slowly turned. But while doing so, he thought, in clear microseconds, what am I doing?

He felt lightheaded. Everything now seemed fuzzy, distorted, as if life itself were changing. He felt his grip loosening; he felt as if he were going to topple backward.

Leo struggled to maintain his grip on the doorknob. He squeezed with all his strength, but when he did so, the door pulled violently into him, hitting the side of his head with the sharp edge. The sound was a big, hollow thud.

Goddamn, he thought. What am I doing? He looked around to see who might be watching. He was suddenly scared. Suddenly vulnerable. He put his hand to his forehead. Already he felt a lump, but no blood. Good.

He exhaled and pulled open the door. The Crazy Lady was lying on top of her bed, reading. Her book was on her chest, and she wore her black sweater but had removed her skirt. It lay on the floor next to the bed. She fanned her spread legs with her book. He could see dark stubble on her very white legs and saw the inviting mound of her pubis under her black panties. "Have you fixed the drain?" she said. She had a thick French accent.

For a while they both stared at each other. After all thoughts of fucking began to subside within him, Leo began a more benevolent desire to communicate something profound and sensitive and understanding. He wanted to tell her that he'd never imagined that he would get older and that he would have such a bullshit job and that he would be capable of being so mean to someone he loved as much as Diana. He wanted to tell the Crazy Lady that he felt for her, sympathized with her, and actually even understood why it was that she walked every day. The walking was, really, just as good as anything else one could do. Why not walk? She wasn't harming anybody. But speech wouldn't come. So he nodded his head. And waited for the Crazy Lady to issue some sage advice to him. Something to jump-start his attitude, which was severely wrong, before and after his affair. The old woman seemed to understand something, for her mouth softened, and it seemed to him as if she almost smiled. Still, she said nothing further.

"I'm not a bad person," he said. And he wasn't; he meant her no harm. Yet what was he doing in her house? in her bedroom?

After a time Leo turned around, leaving the woman's room. The black cat stood at the top of the stairs, staring at him. He brushed past the cat, took the stairs two at a time, opened the front door, looked both ways down the street, and then made for his car.

As he drove back down Golden Lantern, he heard a police siren from up the hill. It was getting closer. Leo, his gaze fixed all the time on his rearview mirror, saw a squad car charge over the rise. He immediately slowed, took from his pocket the small paper that the coke was in, and threw it onto the grass island that separated traffic.

The squad car was on him in an instant. It crowded him from behind as if it wanted to ram Leo's car. Then it quickly veered around and drove down toward the coast.

Leo exhaled as if he'd run a race. He wiped his forehead. Looking once again in the rearview mirror and seeing nothing, he turned right at Pacific Coast Highway, finally heading for his secure condo.

When he arrived home, he parked outside the garage. He wanted to feel the night air. Climbing the spiral stairs that led to his deck outside the bedroom, he smelled the heavy aroma of salt. A slight onshore wind pushed its way from the sea. He heard the breaking waves across the highway.

Leo felt lonely and he hated it and he wondered why he fought so much with Diana, why they were unable to have children, why they weren't enough somehow for each other.

He felt ill. Going inside the old woman's house already had a movie quality about it, and Leo felt as if he'd only been watching one. The cocaine was wearing off. His head ached from all the beers he'd drunk and from the wine. As the waves crashed beyond Coast Highway, the shoreline lit up with phosphorescent explosions.

Shaking his head, Leo now noticed that the sliding door to the bedroom was open. He wearily walked inside the dark. After his eyes adjusted, he saw that Diana was in bed, asleep. She lay on top of the covers with her bright pink silk dressing gown open, revealing her legs—those big legs he loved.

If he wasn't a bad person, what about all the mean things he'd said and might still say to her? All the things that had hurt her, made her feel invaluable. He suddenly felt sorry for her having married him. He wanted tears to form in his eyes but they wouldn't. What mattered was that it shouldn't be this way.

He made his way to the bed and, sitting on its edge, watched Diana, his wife, asleep with her gentle mouth open, the most amazing sight the world had to offer him.

Turning
Mean

Henry was outside playing with his girlfriend; she played domestic scenes with dolls while Henry staged elaborate war games with action figures. The desert air was clear and warm, even for December. Lois, Henry's mother, called for him to come in.

"You get in right now, Henry, and get ready," she yelled down the small strip that separated our apartments from others across the way. I was reading, but mostly I was looking out the window because I couldn't concentrate.

"I don't want to," Henry yelled back.

"You get your little ass in now!" his mother screamed.

"You're fat," Henry yelled back. "Fat, fat, fat!"

Lois *was* fat, but she was also quick, and she ran him down like a sprinter with a sudden burst of speed. Henry slid on the ground, trying to squirm out of her grasp. When he squirmed too much she picked him up by his britches and slammed him to the grass.

"Now you get your little butt in."

Defeated, Henry picked himself up and started to

walk to his apartment, which was next to mine. He put his thumb in his mouth and began a barely audible sob. When Henry began to cry, his girlfriend picked up a toy, offering it to him as a totem. Henry sobbed with his thumb in his mouth and put his free arm over his girlfriend's shoulder as they walked by my window. You could say this for them: they were in it together.

We were married in August. By Thanksgiving my wife had split. She returned to her parents' house. I should have known that it wouldn't last; her parents hadn't wanted us to marry. Her father, in a magnanimous display of speech—he wouldn't talk to me directly—told me I should marry one of my own kind. I answered that I wanted to marry a woman, not a man. He failed to see humor in our exchange, as he failed to see humor in anything because he had no sense of humor. In spite of them, we eloped to Yuma and then continued on to Tucson so that I could attend graduate school. When my wife called her parents, her father wouldn't speak to her, her mother asked why she wanted to live in the desert—they were from an affluent beach community in California—and her brother yelled out that his sister was being raped.

The odd connection about the younger brother yelling rape was that a real live rapist was captured the day my wife left, so those two events will always be connected in my memory. This guy was dubbed the "gift-giving" rapist by local media. He'd been serving a forty-year prison term for rape when he escaped. He would rape his victims and then give them a small gift, a cheap necklace, an inexpensive ring, a box of candy, anything. He was arrested in the university library, reading a book on jazz, and he waved to the cameras like a celebrity.

I stayed on in married student housing after my wife's departure because there was a feeling of comfort and of family, even though I had neither. The project wasn't much to look at, really an army base impersonation with a few palm trees lining the outside of the complex. Some random maples were scattered about on the inside, their leafless limbs making for an even starker look over the dead winter grass. The buildings were low and constructed of hollow block, creating a family-like familiarity because of the common walls. You could hear everything.

My neighbors on one side were Egyptian, and they made love every Tuesday and Sunday nights on the bathroom floor. They were quite regular. Most of the other nights the woman cried.

Henry and Lois were my neighbors on the other side. Through the hollow block wall, I usually heard the television set turned off around midnight. Henry slept right next to it. He turned on cartoons around six in the morning. Lois was studying criminology and believed in letting Henry make up his own mind about things. What shows to watch, what time to go to bed, what music to listen to.

Lois's husband had raped her when they were estranged. Henry was the product of that violation. And that was why Lois was studying criminology. She hadn't taken kindly to the term "date rape" in regards to her estranged husband's attack, nor did she feel respect toward people who claimed that it was a family matter in the first place. She now wanted to make a difference.

It's funny how you can tell a stranger things you wouldn't tell someone else. I had told Lois all about my wife's family. We were, after all, both students, struggling to survive academia.

On Sunday, instead of studying as I should have been, I watched the football game on TV with Henry. We ate ice cream while yelling at the players.

"That's my father," Henry said, his small six-year-old body wriggling off the couch as Walter Payton outran everyone for a touchdown.

"I doubt it," Lois said, walking up to my open door. "C'mon

home now, honey," she said to Henry. "You ready for your haircut, Jesse?"

Actually, Jesús is my name, but everybody called me Jesse. I had agreed to watch Henry for Lois while she finished a paper. She was to give me a haircut; she used to cut in a salon.

"Thanks for the 'scream,'" Henry said.

He handed me the bowl. I put his bowl and mine on the coffee table that I was still paying for. Because my wife had taken a liking to it, we gave up a perfectly good table that I made during my Japanese period. I turned off the television.

All three of us marched next door. Lois took a chair from her dinette and set it in the small kitchen that had a linoleum floor. She removed some dirty dishes from the sink, disappeared into the bathroom for shampoo, then returned and adjusted the water temperature. "Okay, Jesse," she said.

I leaned over the sink, staring down into the strainer, letting warm water flow over my aching head. A thin, washed-out piece of spaghetti and a faded former lettuce leaf swirled under the pressure of the water. Immediately Lois's strong and reassuring hands kneaded my scalp. She said she liked to cut my hair because it was thick and wavy and it always looked good after the cut. After she washed it, she dried it somewhat and then wrapped a towel around my neck and shoulders. I sat in the chair.

"You hear from your wife?"

Henry turned on the television, but instead of watching the game as I hoped he would, he tuned it to MTV—they had cable—just as Paula Abdul was prancing about in her lingerie. Henry began dancing with the video. My wife really liked to dance too.

"No." I didn't tell Lois that I had written three times, never receiving an answer.

"Sometimes there's too many things against it," she said as she moved around me, deftly snipping here, snipping there with her small scissors that had a tong on the round part of the handle.

I wondered about her husband. Lois hadn't used the word

"rape" when she told me about Henry's conception. She had said, "forced himself." As I watched Henry playing in front of the tube, I wondered what his father looked like. Henry had soft freckles, was solid as a brick shithouse, and Lois had razor-cut a part in his hair.

My wife and I were going to have children, two of them. "It was her parents," I said lamely.

"As soon as the holidays come, people start yearning for their own." Lois had sworn off men. She wanted no relationships.

Henry cranked up the volume, moving to a Prince video.

"Hey, turn that down, you fool."

He turned it down, a bit.

Lois took strands of my hair in each of her hands and measured them against each other. She took her squirt bottle, doused the front of my hair, and then cut off some more. She did her measurement number again, this time satisfied, for she removed the towel from my neck, slapped at the hair on my face, and said, "That's it."

I went to the pantry and took her broom to sweep.

"That's okay. I got someone else coming over."

Next door at my apartment, I showered (I hate those hairs that get stuck in the collar of your shirt) and then studied all evening. Around ten, after my neighbors had made love (their bathroom was right next to my desk), the phone rang.

"What's all the noise?" I asked my wife.

"I'm at a club," she said

I could tell that she'd been drinking. There was a long, long silence.

"I want to see you at Christmas. I want to talk."

I didn't much like the fact that she was going out. "I'll talk."

"But I'll tell you right now, I'm never going back to Arizona as long as I live," she said.

"That sort of limits the options, doesn't it?"

She said she still wanted to be married, but she didn't want me in school. Her father would "give" me a job. They must have worked out some compromise, something that I wasn't even a part of. Maybe I was being foolish. Maybe things were as her father said, I would never get anywhere, in the end.

I stayed up almost the entire night, finally falling asleep on the couch before dawn. It was around ten in the morning when I took out my trash. My eyes burned and everything that I looked at had an edge to it, a hard one.

The trash bin was next to the parking lot. Trash was collected often enough, but people were too lazy to throw their refuse in the large bin. They simply dropped it in front, and as a result, there was always trash blowing around the parking lot.

I watched my next-door neighbor walk up in his full-length white muslin dress and drop his trash in front of the bin.

"Hey," I yelled to him, "why don't you put your trash *in* the bin?"

"And why don't you mind your own business?" he asked me in his over-enunciated British accent.

"We're not all peasants here," I said.

One thing led to another and I finally told him to go back to bum-fuck Egypt if he didn't like the way things were here. He pushed me, we threw a few blows, but it wasn't much of a fight. Yet it felt good to hit somebody.

As it turned out, some of the children had been watching. When I passed them on my way back to my apartment, they screamed, "Run, here comes the mean man!"

The days raced by, and I was lost in work. I hadn't been to school in many years, so it was extra hard for me. And every time I walked down the parkway to my apartment, all the children fled, screaming, "It's the mean man!" It had become a sort of game for them. Except it wasn't amusing for me.

The weekend after the scuffle, I fixed a flat tire for Henry. I asked him if he knew how to work on bikes.

"Naw, I only work on cars," he told me.

"How long has it been flat?"

"Two years," he answered.

He was lying, since I had seen him tearing through the complex, showing off for the other kids, trying to stand on the cross bar of the bike while it was moving, and once bailing off it while going quite fast. He hadn't been hurt either of those times. But his tires had air in them.

So we drove over to the Target discount store for a patch kit. Henry immediately went into the record department to see if Paula Abdul's new album was out. For some reason I found myself in the outdoor section looking at BB guns, thinking of all the children mocking me, calling me mean. I *was* feeling mean.

But I finally rounded up Henry, found a patch kit, and drove back home. When we walked up from the parking lot, the children were playing in a group. They stopped their game and one girl screamed, "Run! Mean man!"

Before they were able to scatter, Henry took hold of my hand and bellowed out, "He's my friend."

We casually strolled by the children, insulated in the warmth of each other's hand.

School was already out for the elementary school children as I was taking my finals. I had been up almost the entire night finishing a paper, had taken a two-hour final at school, and was returning home when I stumbled upon the most horrible scene I have ever experienced.

The sprinkling of maples lining our parkway had lost almost all their leaves. It was a black and white December day, a thin, high overcast graying everything. And it was cold. So cold you could see your breath.

On one of the trees someone had installed a rope with a tire hanging from it so the children could swing. I didn't know what the children were doing out in this weather, but there they were, gathered around the tree with the tire, gathered around Henry, who had somehow become entangled with the rope so that it was tight around his neck and he was dangling there like a second tire.

His short stubby legs kicked, his entire body squirmed, struggled, his little legs flailed valiantly. He fought like a tiger.

It took me just a second to assess the situation. And for some reason the rope triggered rape in my mind. Rope. Rape. And then I sprang.

In five days it will be Christmas. I'm going home. I'm going to talk with my wife. Henry gave me a bottle of Aqua Velva aftershave for a present. I gave him a football. Henry and Lois were going to Phoenix for the holidays. I helped them with their presents and suitcases to the car, pushing the shopping cart Lois had loaded them in.

"Are you comin' back?" Lois asked me.

"I really don't know," I said.

Henry walked in front of us, skipping and throwing his new football high in the air.

"She don't love you. She'd be here if she did," Lois said.

I didn't answer her. We walked out to their beat-up car. Trash covered the parking lot. Henry got inside the car and took off his jacket as we loaded the gifts in the trunk on top of the suitcases. Lois got in the car and started it up. It was a faded blue Olds with a rubber strip hanging from the dented bumper as if it had been maimed in a fight.

After I moved the shopping cart, she backed the car up, softly crunching gravel.

Henry, who had been in the back, jumped over the bench seat and leaned on Lois so he could get his head to the open window. He wore a clean white turtleneck, and he looked like a very young skier just before he goes down the hill, or like a small golfer on a very cold day, keeping warm before teeing off, or like a tennis player after an invigorating game, cooling off.

"MERRY CHRISTMAS!" he yelled to me.

"Shut up," Lois said. "You yelling right in my ear. Ain't you got no pride?"

Lois smiled her warm smile at me and Henry kept yelling Merry Christmas as the car pulled away, until his voice no longer carried in the endless desert twilight.

La Luz

When the snowflake fell, I'd almost laid out the entire house. It descended slowly, like a lost feather out of a down pillow, its form palpably magic. We didn't get snow this far south, this close to the ocean in California. But there it was, a solitary snowflake, changing form before my eyes, turning from a frozen crystal into a wet imprint on the wood.

I looked up. Everything was gray. And I could see my breath exploding before me in small puffs. Saws were going on other slabs, guys framing. The cutoff saw still whirred its hollow, reassuring echo, and farther back on the tract the plasterers' hopper droned as it spat "mud" on lathed houses. I could smell the aromatic scent of wet fir being sliced over and over as we fashioned three-dimensional puzzles in space, and I could smell the wild pungent aroma from the surrounding fields, even now smell the oranges from the grove. The trees drooped, laden with fruit, orange Christmas decorations sparkling against dusty leaves, glowing, almost, in the gloominess of the day. Putting my hammer in my bag, I saw the snowflake half disappear into the two-by-four on which I'd made my last layout mark.

From out of the orange grove, farther down the dirt street where only the bottoms were framed, came two *paisanos*. I wouldn't say wetback nor illegal alien, though you might. I was sure they were from *el otro lado*. What was the big deal? Everyone working around me was from somewhere else—the East Coast, the Midwest, Asia, Europe, Latin America. As they got closer I could tell that one of them was a woman. She carried a small, faded-brown overnight satchel with both hands clutching the leather handle, and she had dark hair tied in a ponytail, which floated around as she walked.

A woman out here was odd. We didn't have them, except for the catering truck drivers. This was Little League in the old days, Pop Warner, topless bars, and the Baja 500 all rolled into one male mindset. Maybe she was labor like the rest of us, I thought, watching them enter our outpost at the base of San Joaquin Mountain.

The man was tall and wore dark slacks with a fleece-lined jacket. He even had black ski gloves. The woman wore faded Levi's and a white blouse covered by a thin red and blue blanket-shawl that crisscrossed her chest and hung almost over her arms. On her feet she wore sandals with thick gray homespun socks. She was short and solid, built to work.

The man would forge ahead, leaving the woman behind, and then he would turn, pulling her up even with him. She resisted his touch subtly and stubbornly, for she continued to slow him down, as if she were either very tired or very willful. I knew there was a trail from the border through the backside of the Murietta Forest, which we were on the west edge of, so I figured maybe the woman had walked the trail. She appeared exhausted.

They marched past me, the man in the lead, the woman following, up to a fire that had old cars around it. Landscapers surrounded the fire, heating coffee. The man and woman had words for a moment, seeming to disagree strongly. After they stopped yelling, the man in the fleece-lined jacket approached the circle of men. He pointed to the woman and said something, which brought laughter from the men. The woman turned away, staring up in the sky. Our gazes locked for just a second, but she quickly looked away, out into the fields.

I looked there too. Tracts were springing up all around us, sort of like a twentieth-century gold rush. Scrapers and earth movers graded quadrants for more houses; shopping centers would follow. Looking back at the landscapers' fire, I saw that the man in the fleece-lined jacket now had a beer. The woman had put her suitcase on the ground and cupped a steaming drink in her hands, sipping from it, yet nodding and then waking with a quick jerk. Someone else, another man, helped her to the fire. Her brown satchel remained outside their circle, looking lost and dingy.

As I scanned the entire tract, I felt a feeling of peace and familiarity. There was a sense of humanity here—the new arrivals were welcome. And we were bonded in work as we gave it our all in fields that would soon become neighborhoods. Yet none of the workers would ever live in these instant affluent communities. But that was okay.

These houses were a huge contradiction. Casterbridge Estates, Phase III. They would start at a quarter million. And that would be for the few single stories. The 3 Plan, the one I was rolling second-story ceiling joist for, would sell for half a million. A lot of the laborers lived in the hills, walking to work, sleeping in the brush, making do with plywood and cardboard lean-tos, or else living in their cars, like Johnny Fasthorse, the guy who built all the kitchen soffits. Lots of guys in the trades were living on the job.

I looked where I'd made my last keel mark. No more snowflake. Mount Joaquin was lost in the mist. Everything was pressed down, the way I felt. So carry on. Don't stop moving. Not when you're in the air, for if you think, then you look down, and if you look down, you fall.

And the incredible thing about the fall is how fast the ground comes up to meet you. Thirty-two feet per second squared. It's one of a few completely fair systems, the same for everyone. You think you'll have time to figure things through, but you won't. It's too fast. So there it is, you and the ground will meet. It's just a matter of time.

No more snowflakes fell, so I started spreading, taking the first boards, which, if the loads were built correctly, would be the ones I needed, to the farthest end of the house. Somehow you walk on top of that three-and-one-half-inch plate, your toes gripping as much as they can through your tennis shoes, with the joist, an eighteen-foot-long two-by-six, balanced in your arms so that it has equal weight on either side of your body, making you a bit like the tightrope walker, except he has a pole. Not looking down, you walk: one foot over the other, a game of balance, all the way to the edge of the building. On the perpendicular wall you set one end of the joist down while still holding the other end cradled underneath your arm. Then wiggle the board across the wall until it has spanned the room. Lay it on its side and go back for another. Each successive joist gets easier, for you can balance just a second in between the board you've already laid down. After you've spread the room, you have a bunch of sagging joist ready to be rolled.

That was what I did. Mark layout, spread material, roll, block, and cut specials. And since Christmas was almost here, I wasn't working a full day because we were having a party. Efren, one of the stackers, the guys who build roof structures, was across the street stirring *carnitas* in his big copper vat, using a rowboat oar to jostle the meat.

Even from my high vantage point I could hear the crackle of the fire underneath the vat, smell the hot food wafting up toward me. I supposed that *carnitas* from Efren was as close as we'd get to a formal Christmas party, which was okay.

Still, a sense of excitement rode down the streets on small wings of wind, raising everyone's expectations, making us concentrate on anything but the "now," which wasn't all that great.

After I'd rolled the upstairs master bedroom, the second bedroom, and the upstairs den, all I had left were the front two bedrooms. Usually I finish a house while I'm on it rather than setting up again. But I was excited about the party, so I figured if I pushed to finish this house the work would diminish quality-wise. And I hated that, which was why I worked alone, hand-nailing. No compressor and nail gun, no partners, no slave illegal labor. Just my bags and saw and cord. That was it. Light and quick. Agile. Accurate. I took responsibility for my work. I took pride in it, never leaving a house until it was done to *my* satisfaction. The only way to make progress in this world, I knew.

Nobody had taken lunch because we were stopping early, and besides, the catering truck woman wasn't due back until after Christmas. I didn't know how the guys knew the food was done, but more and more men gathered around Efren's fire, drawn to the cooking meat.

The plasterers had stopped, the saws around the tract were falling silent, the job was winding down for the day, even the ubiquitous heavy metal tract music ceased. In spite of the cold, everyone was drinking beer. I blew in my cupped hands, looking for the woman. She was now sitting before the landscapers' fire, her arms folded over her knees, head down, asleep. I pulled up the hood on my sweatshirt.

Before I lowered my saw down, I watched Efren spear a piece of meat from the vat. With his big Bowie knife he placed the steaming pork on a two-by-twelve scrap and then daintily tasted a small chunk. He yelled something I couldn't' hear, and his brother came stomping out of a house with a platter.

From the same house I heard yelling and whooping, and I could see color shadows jumping from the hole where the sliding glass doors would eventually go, sometime in the not-too-distant future. Even from high up and across the street I could hear the repetitious moans and pseudo-romantic music accompanying the pornography they were watching. Oh, man. But I had already paid my ten bucks for beer and food, so what the hell? I could get some hot meal and then go home.

Plenty of time to be alone. That was the hardest part of no longer being married. The time alone. And the quiet. All I'd ever wanted was love, yet it seemed I couldn't have it. Maybe it was quite a lot to ask.

"You working all day?" the Cowboy Nazi, who had materialized on the slab below me, shouted. He wore an old Mackinaw hunting jacket and cowboy boots and a black cowboy hat. He carried a pint of Jack Daniels.

"Every fucking day," I answered without looking at him. I didn't like the Cowboy Nazi. His tattoos had color in them, done at a parlor. All the other guys' tattoos were black, prison tattoos.

After he walked off I lowered my saw to the slab. Across the way a buzz of chatter slowly rose. The owner of the framing company had arrived. He would have our money and, if we were lucky, some sort of bonus. I remembered the years they'd given us hams or turkeys, but now they gave us green. Everything was money. What could I do with a turkey anyway?

I climbed down the brace material in the wall, stepping diagonally, as if I were using a ladder. After pulling my cord out of the house, I stretched it tightly from the power pole and began forming big, slack loops.

Maybe the reason I was joisting was because few tools were needed. A saw, a cord, a set of bags, and nails. They supplied the nails. The saw and cord and bags fitted in the front of my car, all I really owned. A '61 Porsche Super Ninety with a sunroof.

When I loaded my *chingaderas* in the trunk, I put on my leather jacket over my sweatshirt and looked up at the sky. It was all gray and silent. That thing that had fallen must not have been snow, I thought.

Approaching Efren and the food, I heard shouting and laughter from the house behind him.

"Get *una plata*," Efren said to me.

"Did you see any snow?" I asked him, taking in a big hit of smell from the simmering vat. I stood close to Efren, almost touching him, warming my hands over the fire.

He stirred in a slow, hypnotic, clockwise motion. The lower part of the oar was all white, the varnish cooked off. He looked at me blankly, as if he were having some sort of mystical communion with the pork in the simmering vat. Efren said, "Al's got a bottle."

At the side of the house, next to the porno room, a group of guys surrounded Al, the foreman. A small paper sack moved among them.

I walked over. "Did you guys see any snow?"

Spot, who had a great red birthmark covering the left half of his face, shook his head.

Little Magua, a laborer, sauntered up and, as if he'd heard my question, said, "Dr. George says snow."

"That weatherman don't know shit from Shinola," Grizzly said. Grizzly was hairy and big. His face was covered with hair, and his hands were as large as bear paws, the tops covered with fur, all the way to his knuckles.

Al handed me the paper sack. He was tall and clean shaven, with a chiseled chin. He wore faded boots with new Dockers and a polo shirt with a red down parka. His hands were clean, though callused.

I took a swig from the sack, letting the brown delicious warmth glide down my throat.

"You ain't got AIDS, Jess?" the younger of the Gold Dust Twins asked. Three thick gold chains flopped on his chest, over his jacket.

I flipped him the bone.

"Dr. George is full of shit up to his ears," Johnny Fasthorse said. He wore his hair long and braided, and was homeless, living in the orange grove in his car. His hands had an orange tint to them from all the oranges he ate.

"I saw snow," I said, passing the sack to Al.

"It's cold enough to snow," Grizzly said.

"More money!" Julio shrieked from the porno room. He'd been decorated in Vietnam.

Al took a nice slow drink from the sack, watching everyone.

Efren carried another full platter into the house as guys from the other trades milled about. Plasterers by the sliding glass opening, wearing their splattered whites with down jackets over them, drinking beer; roofers out by a dually, sharing their own bottle; drywallers, their hands chalky white from handling board all day, in the garage next door, smoking pot; plumbers, their hands permanently flux stained, drinking by one of the coolers filled with beer; and even a bunch of landscapers had returned to the fire out by the grove, but no longer was the woman with them.

"What are all these guys doing here?" Little Magua asked.

"They paid their ten bucks," Spot said. "Who cares?"

"More money for the craps game," the oldest Gold Dust Twin said.

After eating there would be gambling. A lot of cash would be floating around, especially with fifty, sixty guys getting paid green plus Christmas bonuses.

"More money!" Julio yelled again.

The Owner glided effortlessly between plasterers, shaking his head in reaction to the taunt from Julio.

"The baby needs milk," Spot chimed in.

"As long as the eagle shits," Efren yelled in Spanish from across the dirt street.

"I've got your money," the Owner said, reaching into his breast pocket, stretching his camel hair coat tightly so you could see the bulge of his pistol.

I used to run work, even had my own company, employing fifteen guys, and I used to pay in cash too. But packing a gun was one thing I refused to do.

"You guys working tomorrow?" the Owner asked. "You, Jess?" He smelled like Old Spice aftershave.

He knew I always did. I had nothing else. "It's going to snow."

After most everyone had eaten, Big Martian started a fire right on the slab in the garage. Smaller Martians built a backstop for craps. Those Martians were thieves and they loved money and they would get it by any means.

Immediately the garage filled with guys hoping to multiply their fortunes. Only one adjective goes with money: more. And here's the thing, only a few people can ever have a lot of money. Some sort of cosmic law, like gravity or something. One or two guys would win big, most of the others would lose some, and a few would lose big. And those were the ones to avoid, the big losers, because they would, in all likelihood, try to get their money back. They would make the most noise, be the most physical, drink the most. In short, they were the biggest assholes.

The Martian without a shirt was a major ass, but he had a whole baseball team of relatives backing him, so he wasn't such a loser after all. They were all from Florida, brought here in migratory waves by Big Martian, who was a siding pimp and would hire outsiders only as a last resort. They flew Confederate flags in front of all the houses they sided. The Martian without the shirt dropped to his knees on the garage slab and yelled to the afternoon sky, "Come to papa, yeah!" as he rolled the dice. Snake eyes. The loser as bait.

A drywall man stepped up with green in his hand and said, "Let's go, baby."

They rolled. And the clinks of the dice were compounded by the cold, drawing everybody into a tight circle.

Out front Efren was cooking the last batch of *carnitas*, talking to a few latecomers. The porno moaning kept a steady beat, highlighted by sporadic yelling from the garage slab, where the craps game was gathering momentum.

I'd drunk some beers and had numerous hits off whiskey bottles and eaten a hot meal, such as it was. But more important, I was with people.

The clouds had completely deserted the twin humps of Mount Joaquin, making it almost glow from the snow on the very top. A thin streamer cloud blew off the tip as if it were a banner.

While I gawked at the mountaintop, suddenly applause and shouts filled the air. A lot of guys ran toward the garage slab, joining the bulging crowd. Their bodies pushed in and then fell away, like a tidal surge against sea rocks.

At first I thought a fight had started, although in all my years working I'd never actually seen one. But they did occur. This thought quickly disappeared when I heard the gravelly voice of Big Martian yell, "You can buy a WOMAN!"

Upon hearing such a strange idea, I, too, hustled over to the side of the garage, behind which the backboard had been set up, and pushed my way onto the slab. And there, much to my dismay, stood the woman I had seen earlier, for sale.

"Liver," Big Martian said. "Who wants a woman?"

"She ain't even awake," Spot said.

And she wasn't. The man in the fleece-lined jacket propped her up. But in spite of her unconscious state she still clutched her small suitcase.

"You can't buy and sell people," I said.

The Owner said, "I'm history." He split.

"This guy wants to sell her," Big Martian said.

We all looked at the man in the fleece-lined jacket. He stood behind the woman, supporting her, saying something in Spanish that I couldn't quite hear because of all the commotion.

Efren translated and shouted: "He says, 'She's very tired.' "

No shit. But there was something more, there always was.

"I'll give ten bucks," a drywall man shouted.

"The strippers will be here soon." Al was trying to divert attention.

"They're not coming," Grizzly said.

"I think I'll buy her and fuck her 'til she begs for mercy," Waylon Willie said.

"Easy," Al said.

"Let's all chip in and buy her and then we can have a train," Spot said.

"Shut up," I said to Spot.

"Who knows what diseases it's got," the Cowboy Nazi said.

"Shut the fuck up, you moron," I said to Cowboy Nazi.

The man in the fleece-lined jacket spoke with Efren, who then announced that only one man could buy her.

"What gives him the right to sell her?" I asked.

"He's her husband," Efren said.

That quieted some of the meaner ones in the crowd. Even they knew something serious was happening.

I came back with "So?"

Efren looked at me with squinted eyes, as if he were trying to interpret something beyond his realm of reason.

"I'll get her alone, then," Grizzly said. "Twenty."

"Gash!" someone yelled.

"Is this guy serious?" Al asked Efren.

"I think so."

Al threw up his hands and said, "Forget it." He left the garage slab.

"Twenty-five," Little Magua said.

A roofer chimed in with thirty.

The bidding was serious, everyone wanting to see how far it would go. See if things would get out of hand.

"That's too much for a fucking spic," Cowboy Nazi said.

"Hey, white trash," Efren said to Cowboy Nazi.

"Knock it off," Julio said in his deepest voice. He was big, almost as large as Cowboy Nazi. "No fighting on the job."

"Thirty-five," a plasterer said.

"He don't want her no more," Spot said with glee.

Trying to get eye contact with anybody, I said, "You've got to stop this shit."

A yell from Grizzly upped the bid fifty bucks.

"You can stop it with *money*," Big Martian said to me.

I didn't know why, but I thought of my own life and about all the times I'd acted wrongly, or even worse, the times I'd not acted at all. So without realizing the implications of my words, I said, "Two hundred."

A few "whoas" passed through the crowd, followed by laughter. And everything seemed suddenly colder, clearer, and slower.

Big Martian said, "Any other bids?" Nobody responded. To me he said, "You bought yourself a woman."

"I've heard of this in Peru, but never here," Fermin said.

Big Martian grabbed my hundred-dollar bills.

"Enema!" the Cowboy Nazi yelled.

"Helmut, yeah!" Waylon Willie added.

"Hand it over," I said to Big Martian.

Julio snatched my money from Big Martian and said, "Let's finalize this thing."

"Let's shoot some fucking craps," Grizzly said.

The man in the fleece-lined jacket grabbed the woman by her wrist, pulling her forward, waking her. We followed Julio off the garage slab, out front by Efren's now smoldering fire.

Al leaned against his truck. "Now what?"

"I'll get my money back," I said. "Thanks for your help."

Al shrugged.

"It's not done that way," Efren said.

Efren, Efren's brother, Al, and Johnny Fasthorse surrounded Julio and me. The woman was trying to speak with her husband, but he would have nothing to do with her.

"He's right," Julio said. "A deal's a deal."

"I don't want to buy somebody."

"You just did."

"C'mon, Al, help me out here."

"I can't. You had to open your big mouth."

"What? And let Grizzly get her?"

"You're the one that got involved. You're the one that stood up for rights," Julio said.

"She's funky," Efren said.

We all stared at the woman. She looked to be in her early thirties. She was short, her gaze unfocused, and she held her head high. Her hair blew around her face as the wind brushed it. The man in the fleece-lined jacket now held the valise.

A huge roar erupted from the craps game.

"I didn't know you were like that," Efren's brother said to me.

"Like what?" I said.

Efren came up close to me, whispering, "She's got a big toilet." To his brother he said, "Get the copper pot. I want to split before them rednecks really get going."

Oh, shit, I thought. "Look, Julio, I just wanted to talk some sense into that asshole," I said, pointing to the man in the fleece-lined jacket. "I didn't want to buy his wife."

"What do you want I should do? This man put her up in good faith." He, too, gestured to the man in the fleece-lined jacket. "Now you want to break the deal? Where would we be without a word?"

I didn't want to hear that sort of bullshit. "You know in your heart that it's wrong for one person to sell another."

"No, it's not."

"We had a war over it. The Civil Fucking War." I looked at Al for verification. He nodded approval.

"These guys aren't Americans."

Julio had me there. "But we are."

"That war don't mean shit to me," Johnny Fasthorse said.

"Maybe we could sell her for a profit," Efren said. "Clean her up, know what I mean?"

"I used to think you were okay, Efren," I said.

"Little Magua will give you twenty-five," Efren's brother said. He closed the back flap on Efren's SUV.

"Why?" I yelled at the husband. *"Por qué?"*

He snickered and said, *"Aquella es malvada."*

"How bad can she be?" I asked.

"She ain't bad," Efren said, starting his rig. He revved the engine. "She's evil," he said, smiling. His rear tires crunched a two-by-four as he pulled away.

"Don't start that shit," I said.

"Why so glum?" Julio said. "You've got a woman." He handed the money to the man in the fleece-lined jacket.

"Don't," I said, making for them. Julio placed himself between me and the man in the fleece-lined jacket.

"Got to," Julio said.

"Have fun," Al said. He started his truck.

"Wait," I said to Al, hoping for a chance to grab the man in the fleece-lined jacket and hoping, too, for some help from my friends.

"What do you want me to do?"

"I don't want to be a part of this."

"You already are. Butch it out."

"Christmas is coming up," I said, as if that, somehow, made any difference.

"You want me to take her home? My wife would just love that."

"Why not?"

Al shook his head. "Have fun," he said again, driving off.

When I looked for the man in the fleece-lined jacket, I caught a glimpse of him entering the orange grove. As I started after him, Julio and Johnny both restrained me.

Fermin walked out to us from the craps game and said, "I've got some poems in my car."

"Shut up, Fermin."

"No, man, she'll like them."

"Get lost." I shook myself free from Julio and Johnny Fasthorse.

Johnny threw up his arms, said, *"Hasta,"* and walked off.

I heard a car start out in the grove, then saw a trail of dust leaving the shelter of trees.

"You shouldn't have got involved," Julio said. He made for his truck, started it, and drove off down the dirt street.

So there we were, the woman and I, standing in the dirt, with the sun almost set, and the air colder and meaner than it had been all day, snowflakes descending all over us, dusting the ground in a white cotton. The yells from the craps game now had an urgency to them that had been lacking previously. I looked at her. Was she a loser? Was I?

"Let's go," I said, gently.

She yawned. "*Soy Luz.*"

As the snow now fell for real, I thought, I know, and knew why I'd done what I'd done, knew that everything previous in my life had led to this one moment.

Acknowledgments

"In the South" was first published in *Quarterly West* and was a Pushcart Prize XVIII Special Mention. It was reprinted in *Iguana Dreams: New Latino Fiction.*

"My Grandfather's Eye" was first published in *Saguaro.*

"Easy Time" was first published in *Pieces of the Heart: New Chicano Fiction.*

"Turning Mean" was first published in *Blue Mesa Review.*

"La Luz" was first published in *Mirrors Beneath the Earth: Short Fiction by Chicano Writers.*

Further acknowledgments:
Special thanks to Dean Jorge Garcia, School of Humanities, California State University, Northridge. Thanks to the Research, Grants, and Creative Activity Committee, CSU, Northridge, for reassigned time used to write stories in this collection. *Abrazos* to Bruce McAllister for his help with conceptual revision. And last, a hearty thank you to Patti Hartmann for sticking with the manuscript.

About the Author

Jack Lopez was born in Lynwood, California. He is the author of *Cholos & Surfers* and is a professor of English at California State University, Northridge, where he teaches creative writing.